"About that

"I apologize." Lucie felt herself color warmly. "I didn't mean to speak so…abruptly. It was an upsetting day—"

"You were right. I shouldn't have been sitting inside the church while those kids were playing ball right outside. I want St. Andrew's to be the kind of church that has an open door to its community. I'd like the parishioners to feel comfortable about dropping in if they need something…."

She listened, suddenly liking Tanner Bond a whole lot more than she had just minutes before.

"This is my first pastorate. I'm still trying to get that atmosphere started."

It cost Tanner Bond a lot to say that. Lucie wondered what she could do to help this man.

Books by Lyn Cote

Love Inspired

LYN COTE

Lyn lives in Iowa with her husband, her real-life hero. They raised a son and daughter together. Lyn has spent her adult life as a schoolteacher, a full-time mom and now a writer. Lyn's favorite food is watermelon. Realizing that this delicacy is only available one season out of the year, Lyn's friends keep up a constant flow of "watermelon" gifts—candles, wood carvings, pillows, cloth bags, candy and on and on. Lyn also enjoys crocheting and knitting, watching *Wheel of Fortune* and doing lunch with friends. She also enjoys hearing from readers. By the way, Lyn's last name is pronounced "Coty."

THE PREACHER'S DAUGHTER

LYN COTE

Love Inspired

Published by Steeple Hill Books™

STEEPLE HILL BOOKS

Steeple
Hill®

ISBN 0-373-87228-3

THE PREACHER'S DAUGHTER

This edition published by arrangement with Steeple Hill Books.

® and TM are trademarks of Steeple Hill Books, used under license. Trademarks indicated with ® are registered in the United States Patent and Trademark Office, the Canadian Trade Marks Office and in other countries.

Visit us at www.steeplehill.com

Printed in U.S.A.

Jesus replied: "Love the Lord your God with all your heart and with all your soul and with all your mind. This is the first and greatest commandment. And the second is like it: Love your neighbor as yourself. All the law and prophets hang on these two commandments."

—*Matthew* 22:37-40

Chapter One

Late-May sunshine gilded the weathered wood fence around the farmyard. Lucie Hansen leaned against the railing on the wide front porch of the white-frame farmhouse. She wished she'd had time to linger over coffee this morning. But this wasn't a pleasure visit to Pleasant Prairie, Iowa.

Three days ago, her cousin Sophie had called in tears over her husband's continued hospital stay. So Lucie had promised she'd come as soon as she could pack. At that time, Lucie hadn't yet taken in just how deep Sophie's troubles were. Now, three days later, she realized that her cousin's problems might keep Lucie at the farm longer than she'd expected—or wanted. She felt both sorry for her cousin and guilty over feeling selfish. But *she* had problems, too!

Lucie worried her lower lip. *I'm almost broke. I've got to be looking for a summer job and a full-time job for the fall. Lord, You're going to have to help me out here.*

Sophie stood near Lucie, holding her baby daughter on her hip. The girl's dark curls and olive skin matched her pretty mother's.

A riff of heavy-metal music blasted from an open second-story window. Ordinarily, the sound wouldn't have bothered Lucie, fresh from four years in a college dorm. But one glance told her that the raucous sound was upsetting Sophie. And her cousin didn't need any more upsetting right now.

Sophie looked so forlorn, Lucie's mood lowered even further. *Should I offer to go along with her to the hospital?*

"Lucie!" one of Sophie's little boys called to her.

Sophie's young sons already hung on to and twisted themselves around the door handles of Lucie's battered car. The longing in their expressions tugged at Lucie's heart. The little guys couldn't *wait* for Lucie's promised treat of a trip to the town park, to be followed by Dairy Queen hamburgers, fries and cones.

Sophie forced a tiny smile. "Don't worry about me, Lucie."

The heavy-metal music overhead zoomed a decibel louder, drowning out Sophie. Exasperated, Lucie looked upward. What was *with* Zoë, anyway?

Zoë was Sophie's teenaged sister-in-law who'd been living with Sophie and her husband since the death of her parents. Yesterday, Lucie had noted the drastic change in the teen from a year ago. Zoë's low-cut, hip-hugging jeans and exposed navel hadn't bothered Lucie. The desperate unhappiness in Zoë's eyes had.

Shaking her head, Sophie leaned close to Lucie's ear. "I don't know what I would have done if you couldn't have come for the summer."

The summer? I came for the summer? Lucie swallowed this with some difficulty. *When did I volunteer to stay the whole summer?* She hadn't even guessed that Sophie had assumed she'd stay for the entire summer. *I'm broke! I have to find a job!*

Another glance at Sophie's worry-ravaged face made Lucie postpone mentioning this. Sophie was family and family came first. Lucie would have to figure out some way to both help Sophie and find a job. But how?

"*Lu-cie!*" both boys wailed to her in that little-boy please-hurry-up whine.

"I better get going." Lucie hustled down the steps and unlocked what she called "the Bomb," the car that had somehow lasted her through four years of college. "Don't worry, Sophie!" Lucie shouted over her shoulder. "I'll come back in time to drive—" she waved her hand upward to the source of the rock music "—Zoë to work!"

The boys scrambled into the back seat and quickly snapped themselves into their seat belts. Lucie settled herself behind the wheel, turned the key in the ignition and roared down the lane. The roar reminded her, once more, that her father had mentioned she should have her muffler checked. *Oh, well!*

"Is our daddy coming home today?" Danny asked over the rumble of her car.

The unexpected question left Lucie uneasy. *Lord, does he want me to tell him everything will be just like it was before? I can't lie!*

"No, he isn't," Mikey said with audible disgust. "Mommy said Daddy won't come home till he's all better from the accident."

"Oh." Danny subsided.

Lucie didn't wonder that the boys were having difficulty with this situation. Yesterday, visiting their formerly strong and healthy young father in the hospital had shaken her. Out on a county road on his tractor, Nate had nearly died when he'd been hit by a car. It was unbelievable how the irresponsible behavior of one drunk driver could so devastate a man and his entire family.

Poor kids, poor Sophie! Lord, help me help her. And I mean that!

Still, as she drove past fields of black dirt, dotted with green shoots of emerging corn, her spirits lifted. She felt the lingering weight of finals and college graduation drifting away—

A flash of fur. A high yelp.

Lucie slammed on the brakes.

"What happened?" the boys yelled.

She jumped out. "Stay in the car!" Ahead of her,

a small bundle of brown-and-white fur lay crumpled on the asphalt road.

I didn't have time to stop! Dear God, help! She ran to the little animal and knelt down on the sun-warmed road. The dog was conscious. Knowing a wounded animal might snap at her, she began murmuring reassurances. She held her hands in front of his snout to let him smell her. The dog sniffed her hands and then whimpered as though asking for help. Gently she stroked his head. He whimpered more and then licked her hand.

"Poor fella, will you let me help you up?" To gain his trust and to feel for injury or blood, she stroked him soothingly. His heart pounded reassuringly under her palm. When she slid her arms under the dog, he licked her nose. "Okay, fella." Her own pulse pounding in her temples, she lifted him. "Don't worry. I'm going to get you right to the vet."

The few miles flew past, then she whipped through town, turning heads along Main Street. Tall, gray grain elevators loomed ahead, and beyond them the vet's office, a squat cement-block building. A navy blue SUV with the vet's name on its side was parked beside the door. Relief flooded Lucie. *The vet's in!*

Within minutes, Lucie and the white-coated, silver-haired female vet and her assistant hovered over the small dog on the examining table. The anxious boys waited just outside the door on a bench, listening and watching intently.

Then the examination had been done and the treatment was nearly complete. Even though the dog hadn't been seriously injured—no internal bleeding or otherwise damaged organs—Lucie's knees still felt mushy.

The vet finished applying the last of the plaster cast on the dog's front leg. She turned to wash up at the large stainless-steel sink. "You said he darted right in front of you? You're lucky you just clipped him."

"Do you recognize him?" Lucie stroked its shaggy terrierlike fur.

The vet shook her head and lifted the dog into Lucie's waiting arms. "We don't have a license or leash law. Farm dogs are supposed to provide protection and help keep the rodent population down. We have strays in town on and off. I think I've seen this guy near the mobile home court outside town."

Lucie, with Mikey and Danny beside her, followed the vet out to the small linoleumed reception area. Lucie wondered at the barest change in the vet's tone, a slight inflection that denoted disapproval. What was wrong with the mobile home court?

"Hi!" Mikey exclaimed, waving to someone at the doorway across from Lucie.

Lucie glanced over. Just inside the door stood a man with long legs, narrow hips, broad shoulders and…the face of an angel.

A very masculine one with chestnut hair curling around his ears. Dark brows that looked like they had been sculpted by an artist. The planes of his cheekbones—perfection. And an endearing cleft in his chin. *Mmm.*

Cold reality intruded, dropping through Lucie like an ice cube. She was probably ogling—improperly— someone's husband. He must be married. No man that good-looking would remain single over the age of twenty-one. Particularly in a small town like this. And he didn't look like a farmer, either. Was he a school-teacher or principal?

Then she realized that she had "floated" up to him. *What's the matter with me? I'm not fifteen and boy crazy! Good grief! He'll think I'm nuts!* She backed away, stumbled and thumped down onto a bench along the wall in the waiting area.

The stranger gazed down at her as though studying a slide under a microscope.

Noting he didn't wear a wedding band, she took a deep, calming breath.

"Hi, Preacher!" Mikey called out. "What's wrong with your dog?"

The preacher? The preacher! *Good grief—they let men this handsome graduate from seminary now?* His clerical collar should have been a dead giveaway. *How did I miss that?* The man held a teacup-size Chihua-hua. The disparity between the man and his tiny pet hit her funny bone. What a hoot. "*That's* your dog?"

"Yes, this is my dog, Sancho."

His deep voice sent shivers through her.

"Hey!" Mikey, the chatterbox, interrupted, pointing to the dog Lucie held, "This is our cousin Lucie and she hit that dog with the Bomb!"

"Bomb?" he asked, again looking at her, she thought, as he would an amoeba under a slide.

"I lovingly call my car 'the Bomb,'" she snapped, not liking the way he was examining her. "The dog ran out in front of me. I didn't have time to stop."

"I see. Very unfortunate."

"You've brought Sancho in for his flea bath?" the vet interrupted. "Lucie Hansen, this is Tanner Bond, the pastor at St. Andrew's Church."

Lucie offered her hand, thinking that she'd have time to adjust to this man before she attended St. Andrew's with Sophie on Sunday morning.

He shook her hand firmly and then handed his dog over to the vet.

Ignoring the touch of his hand, she looked down at the little dog in her lap and crooned to it. Making herself relax against the rough cement-block wall behind her, she stretched her legs out in front of her. She'd have to get a grip. In this little town, she'd be seeing this man often. She couldn't fall apart like this every time!

Fortunately for her, men didn't always pick up on body language like women did and from Tanner Bond's comments, she didn't think he was more astute about this than the average male. So if she continued cool, calm and collected from now on, he'd never know. Know what? That at their first meeting, he'd turned her already-wobbly knees to jelly?

"So, how badly injured is the dog?" Tanner asked in a kind voice.

"He's going to be fine," the vet answered, handing Sancho to her assistant, who carried it away.

"We just need to find his owner," Lucie put in, wrinkling her brow. She hoped the owner would be understanding. Regret tasted bitter on her tongue.

"I told Lucie that I thought the pooch was from the mobile home court," the vet added.

Again, that hint of disapproval was in the vet's tone. *What am I missing?*

Lucie rose and walked to the counter. "I'd like to drive through there and see if someone claims him. Could you give me directions?" She looked around for a place to put the dog down. When Lucie moved to set the dog on the counter, the vet shook her head. Finally, Lucie turned and plopped the dog into Tanner's arms.

Ignoring his startled expression, she wrote out a check for the vet, subtracting it from her already-low bank balance. *Lord, I need a job. Boy, do I need a job! Maybe You could arrange something part-time around here?*

"I'll go with you to the mobile home court," Tanner offered. "It's just a little out of my way."

Lucie glanced at him. The concern in his eyes could be nothing but genuine. He was a dog lover. "Great. Thanks." She couldn't help but be grateful to have him along when she had to explain the accident to the dog's owner.

She turned to the vet. "How long will this cast have to stay on?"

"Four to six weeks."

A lead sinker dropped through Lucie's stomach. What if she didn't find the dog's owner? She couldn't afford to keep a dog. But maybe she'd be at Sophie's until fall, anyway. *Oh, fudge!*

The vet put the check into a drawer. "If he starts worrying the cast, let me know and we'll rig him up with a collar."

This brought a memory to mind. In spite of her gloom, Lucie almost grinned.

"You find that amusing?" the preacher at her elbow asked.

Lucie shook her head at herself. "Sorry. My sister's cat had to wear one of those collars to keep it from biting and working off a bandage, and the thing looked like a satellite dish around his neck. My brother-in-law called the cat 'Satellite Head' the whole time." And it had driven her sister nuts. *That* had been funny.

Looking at her as if she were a few bricks shy of a load, Tanner handed her back the dog. "I see."

His expression piqued her. *Lighten up, Bond.* Lucie stroked the dog's brown-and-white fur soothingly. The little dog licked her hand again. *You're a sweetie, fella. Hope your owner appreciates you.* "Okay." She let out a deep breath and glanced down at Danny and Mikey. "Let's head for that mobile home court."

"Fine. I'll show you the way." Tanner motioned

for her to precede him out the exit. Mikey and Danny brought up the rear.

Lucy drove behind Tanner's small gray sedan out onto the two-lane highway. In the back seat, Mikey held the dog on his lap. Tanner led them to a mobile home court, named Shangri-La Estates. What a name for a mobile home court in Iowa!

But all was not well in Shangri-La. On the court's sign, someone had spray-painted a neon orange message: ''Go Home Me—'' The last word was nearly undecipherable because the graffiti had been smeared with black paint. Graffiti in Pleasant Prairie? That was weird.

The aging trailers in Shangri-La didn't resemble the shiny new double-wides she saw advertised on TV. Judging from the height of the trees, the court had been here for over twenty years. The shabby office had a Closed sign in its window, so Lucie drove on.

Along the narrow lanes that meandered through the court, most of the mobile homes had dusky Spanish-looking children playing outside. That surprised her, too, though she recalled Sophie saying something about Mexican-Americans moving into town. Had the obscured word on the sign been *Mexicans*—as in Go Home Mexicans?

Ignoring a feeling of foreboding, Lucie parked. Children gathered around her car. Getting out, she carried the groggy dog and approached the nearest trailer that looked and sounded as though someone were home. The nearby children fell silent but trailed behind her. Peering out of the car, Mikey and Danny stared at the other children as if they'd just dropped from the sky. Tanner got out of his car but stayed beside it, watching her. He nodded his encouragement.

His presence heartened Lucie. She marched up the metal steps and knocked on the door. She tried to ignore the quivering in her stomach. When a silver-haired woman opened the door, Latin music poured forth.

"Hello—" Lucie began.

"No hablo inglés," the woman announced with a dour expression.

"Yo hablo español," Lucie said with a grin.

At this, the woman looked startled.

In Spanish, Lucie asked the woman about the dog.

Then, in a mix of Spanish and English, the woman asked what had happened to the dog. Lucie wondered why the woman had said she couldn't speak English when she obviously did. Without betraying this, Lucie explained about injuring the dog and asked again if the woman knew who owned it.

The woman shook her head. "No."

This puzzled Lucie. Something in the woman's expression and manner had led her to believe the woman had recognized the dog. Lucie almost repeated the question, but turned away instead. What was going on here? Was it just that Lucie was a stranger? Or was there already a "history" of trouble between the residents of Shangri-La and the rest of Pleasant Prairie?

Lucie almost assured the woman, "But I'm not from around here."

Scattering children, Lucie walked back to her car.

Tanner met her at her car door. "No luck?"

Distracted, Lucie nodded, trying to think what to do next.

"You speak Spanish?"

"*Sí,* I mean, yes." She looked at the children around her and asked them in Spanish if any of them knew who owned the dog. Again, she got only pensive stares and a few no's. Maybe they'd been told not to talk to strangers? But what kid ever obeyed that?

Tanner was studying her again. "That's very interesting."

Huh? Lucie thought that was a very odd remark.

"What will you do now?" He leaned closer. "Is there any way I can be of help?"

"Thanks, but I can't think of what more to do now." She ignored the clean scent of his soap. "I promised to take the boys to the park, so I guess I might as well."

He nodded. "I have to go back and get Sancho. When you drive out the entrance, just turn left. That will take you back to town."

"Thanks. Bye." Making sure she didn't give the unnerving man a backward glance, she settled the boys and dog in the back seat and headed to town. As she drove, she tried to make sense of the Mexican presence in Shangri-La and wondered if this had been the reason for the vet's odd tone when referring to the trailer court.

At the park on Main Street, the boys jumped out of the car and ran toward the big, old-fashioned metal swing set. This was one of those classic small-town parks, mature trees, green-painted benches, picnic tables and grills, with a baseball diamond at one end and a sanded playground at the other. On the opposite side of the street, near the ball diamond, sat St. Andrew's Church, a brick church with a bright red door.

With the somnolent dog in her arms again, Lucie walked after the boys, admiring the leafy oak trees, spreading like a canopy overhead.

Lucie settled on one of the park benches and laid the dog on her lap. She let the mellow atmosphere soak in. The shade and a gentle breeze kept the flies moving. As she stroked his shaggy fur, the groggy dog licked her hand. Danny and Mikey jumped from their swings and headed for the old wooden seesaw.

"Be careful," she called to them. "I don't want anyone getting a bump on the head. Both of you have your toes on the ground and get off at the same time."

"Okay, Lucie!" they chorused.

She nodded, then looked around. A few Mexican-looking children had gathered on the diamond with a ball and bat. Though lacking two full teams, they began a game of softball. Or they tried.

Most of them looked to be ten years old or less, and they were having trouble finding out which of them could throw the ball far enough to get it over home plate. Lucie watched them as well as Sophie's boys. Before long, Mikey and Danny gravitated to the game.

Dog in her arms, Lucie followed them. "Hi!" she called to the Spanish-looking children. "Need a pitcher?"

They stared at her.

It reminded her of her earlier reception of Shangri-La. "I'm Lucie and this is Mikey and Danny, my cousins." Still no response. She changed languages. She repeated her greeting and introduction in Spanish and then asked, *"¿Necesitan un lanzador?"*

"Sí," the obvious leader, a boy around ten, stepped forward and replied. "Yes, we need a pitcher."

"Okay. What's your name?"

"Miguel." He was stocky with a mop of coal-black hair.

"Okay, Miguel, I'll help. Would one of you please sit and hold my dog while I pitch?" She glanced down at the drowsy dog. The littlest Mexican-American girl came over and took the hurt animal gently into her arms and walked away toward the shade of an oak. Lucie thanked her and then turned back to Miguel. "Let me have the ball. It's been a while, but let's see if I can still get it over the plate."

"Okay, Señorita Lucie." Miguel threw her the ball. His pitch fell short. Noting his chagrin over this, she made no comment.

At first, she practiced a few throws without releasing the ball. Her father's instructions in throwing overhand came back to her. She grinned, remembering her years in softball in grade school. Finally, she drew the ball back overhand and let it go.

It sailed neatly over the plate and all the children cheered. ''Yay for Señorita Lucie! Yay, Lucie!'' the Mexican children and Sophie's boys yelled.

Lucie grinned. ''I guess I haven't forgotten how to pitch. Okay, let's get this game going!''

The children took their places again and Lucie noted that Mikey and Danny were immediately given spots—one on each team.

A glance over her shoulder reassured Lucie that from the little girl's lap, the little dog was watching all of this with sleepy interest. He tried to give them a friendly bark. Lucie waved at him, then she threw her first serious pitch. She struck out the first two players, then a chubby girl hit a foul ball.

The sound of a car pulling in nearby caught her attention. She glanced over to see Tanner Bond with his little dog in hand, walking toward the door to the church's basement. She waved politely. Tanner nodded back formally. Children's voices called her back to the game.

The two boisterous teams battled back and forth with more noise than hits. Lucie remained on the pitcher's mound for both teams, since neither team had anyone else who could get the ball over the plate. The morning sun climbed higher in the sky, and at the top of the sixth inning, Lucie let another ball fly.

At bat, Miguel swung and connected. Crack! The ball shot upward and out of the diamond. The kids on both teams yelled with excitement. It was the first ball that had made it beyond the infield! Lucie jumped high, screaming her encouragement to Miguel. "Run! Run!"

Miguel was halfway to first when the recorded church chimes began to strike the hour—eleven. Lucie took a step back. "Oh, no! I was supposed to get Zoë to work at the DQ by now!"

Miguel made it to second. The children around her clamored for the next pitch as her mind raced. She couldn't let her errand spoil their fun. More importantly, she was making inroads with the people she needed to know to find the dog's owner. Who could help her out here? Tanner Bond walking into church minutes ago popped into her mind. *Yes!*

"*¡Un momento!* Just a sec!" She jogged to the church and into the basement, urgency spurring her. "Hey! Bond! I need you! Hey!"

The man stuck his head out of a door marked Church Office. "Yes?"

"No time to talk! Come on! I need you!" With a hurry-up wave, she headed back outside.

Concern on his face, Tanner hurried out of the basement door after her.

Near the edge of the baseball diamond, she paused to catch her breath and let him catch up. Certainly, he could finish the game for her. She'd only be gone a few minutes. "Hey…kids," she called to the teams, "this…is Tanner Bond, the pastor of that church. He's going to pitch while I run a quick errand. Danny and

Mikey, I have to take Zoë to work. Stay with Mr. Bond! I'll be right back, guys!'' She dropped the ball into his hands.

Tanner caught it, unreality flooding him. *Pitch? Me?* What was she doing? "What? I—hey!"

Ignoring him, she ran to her car. Looking back, she yelled, almost taunting him, "You can pitch, can't you?"

Tanner opened his mouth to insist she come back and explain. But she was already out of range—in her car and speeding out of the parking lot. He glanced down and found himself hip-deep in children, all looking up at him with hope on their faces.

Chapter Two

"So, mister, you gonna pitch or what?" a boy on first base asked with a belligerent twist to his tone.

That twist nearly made Tanner toss back the ball and head back to his quiet office. But he sensed he was needed here. All eyes were upon him. And...perhaps, that woman's parting shot—"You can pitch, can't you?"—stopped him from refusing. "Okay," Tanner mumbled.

"Okay!" the kids shouted with glee.

"Hey, Mikey, you're up!" the kid on base yelled.

But Tanner felt that all attention was on him, not Mikey. Trying to ignore this, he looked around, getting his bearings. Baseball—he hadn't played baseball since...junior high. He gripped the dilapidated leather ball, getting used to the earthy feel of it. *Pitching— I'm the pitcher.* He headed to the pitcher's mound. Then he turned to face Mikey at bat.

"Hey, Preacher," Danny called from behind him, "you can do a few practice throws. Lucie did."

Oh, Lucie had, had she? Tanner grimaced. He raised his right arm and threw the ball.

The ball whizzed past Mikey's nose. Mikey jumped back. "Hey!"

Chagrined with himself for letting his irritation take over, Tanner called, "Sorry! Toss it back."

The same mouthy kid on base called, "Hey! I'm Miguel. You should practice, okay?" Again, that slight twist of contempt crept into the final word. For a kid, Miguel was already working up a sizable chip on his shoulder.

Mikey threw back the ball or rather, dribbled it to a few feet in front of Tanner. He scooped it up and mentally measured the difference between where his ball had gone and where he wanted the next one to go.

"I'm ready," Mikey called.

Tanner clenched his jaw, raised his arm again and let the ball fly. This time it curved away from the plate.

"You gonna call it?" Miguel demanded. "That *señorita* was calling the plays."

"Ball one!" Tanner shouted through gritted teeth. He didn't appreciate *that señorita* putting him in this awkward situation—completely without warning.

"You could just call that a practice throw!" Mikey offered graciously.

"The call stands!" Tanner said, not near ready to

admit defeat. "Here it comes!" He wound up and threw the ball. It flew straight over home plate.

Mikey hit it. It nearly took Tanner's head off. He ducked just in time. The children were yelling and screaming. Miguel and Mikey were running.

His own adrenaline rushing, Tanner spun around, yelling, "Get the ball! Throw me the ball!"

Chasing the rolling ball in the infield, Danny finally captured it and tossed it back toward the pitcher's mound. It dribbled to a stop a few feet to the right of Tanner. Miguel made it home and Mikey halted on third. Tanner walked over and picked up the ball. He faced another player, a girl with dark braids, who was picking up the bat.

"Okay, *padre!*" the girl shouted.

For a moment, just a moment, Tanner thought longingly of the book lying open on his desk. But how could he let the kids down? And evidently, Lucie was off helping Sophie and Nate with Zoë. So if Lucie needed help with the boys, he was happy to oblige, even if it meant doing something he wasn't comfortable with.

Still, Lucie's mocking "You can pitch, can't you?" stuck in his craw. He sucked in a breath and wound up for the next pitch. If she'd only given him some warning....

At the sound of a car door being slammed, Tanner looked over from his spot on the pitcher's mound. Sophie's cousin was back. *Finally!*

"Hey!" she called out, "how's it going?"

"We're having fun, Lucie!" Mikey yelled back.

"*Hola,* Señorita Lucie!" Miguel, along with many of the other children, greeted her.

"How many innings, Tanner?" she asked, pausing at the edge of the diamond.

"We're starting the ninth." *You took long enough.* But he didn't voice this last phrase. And though he'd started enjoying the raucous, slap-dash game, he started to walk toward her.

"No." She held up her hands. "You look like you're doing fine. Go on and finish pitching." She strolled over and sat down on the grass beside the little dog with the cast.

Trying not to notice the carefree swing in her walk, he turned away. He pitched twice more and struck out the batter. Then the recorded church chimes sounded noon.

The teams around him dissolved into kids—yelling to each other and running to bikes, which were propped against trees or lying on the ground.

Retrieving the bat and ball from Tanner and then running to his bike, Miguel called, "Thanks, Señorita Lucie and *padre.* We gotta go! Lunch!"

Within minutes, Tanner and Lucie were left alone with Sophie's boys standing on either side of her and the dog in her arms. Tanner looked at her, irritation trying to rise to his throat but failing.

So she'd interrupted his preparations for his message on Sunday morning. So what? He had to admit his heart was pumping and he was grinning in spite of himself.

But most of all, how could he be aggravated with a woman who looked this good? Earlier, she'd made an impression on him and he still liked what he saw. Below the hem of her modest shorts were a sweet pair of legs, not tanned yet, still pale. Above an athletic-looking body, a round face with an interesting nose, kind of uptilted. Ivory skin already freckling in the sun. Blond curls clustered around her face and her eyes were a tropical blue, an unusual shade.

"So? How did it go?" she asked, obviously sizing him up, too.

"Fine." He still gazed at her, trying to decide why he couldn't look away—even though her offhand, almost brash style annoyed him. She wasn't at all like the young women he usually met in his parish duties. They all treated him with kid gloves.

"Good," she said in a take-charge voice. She looked down, breaking their connection. "Mikey and Danny, head for the car. We're going to go to DQ for lunch, remember?"

"Yippee!" The boys raced each other toward her car.

She straightened herself as though preparing to let him have it.

He braced himself warily.

She looked up at him. "I have one question for you, *Pastor*."

He didn't like the way she emphasized his title. And

why did she sound aggravated? He'd taken her to the mobile home court. He'd pitched in her place. *I haven't done anything to interrupt your morning, Señorita Lucie.* But all he replied was a mild "Yes?"

"What's going on here in Pleasant Prairie?"

That she would ask this hadn't occurred to him. He gave her a puzzled look. "What do you mean exactly?"

"I mean, why are people spray-painting Go Home Mexicans on signs, and what are you doing about it?"

Her unexpected accusation caught him up short. "I beg your pardon?"

"I've only been here three days and I already see that things have changed since my last visit. Changed a lot! When did Pleasant Prairie start becoming Hispanic? And what are you doing to make these newcomers welcome? I—"

"Hold it." He broke into her monologue. "You're *right*—you just got here." He couldn't stand people who sounded off before getting all the facts. "Don't you think you're making a lot of assumptions based on just *one* visit to the mobile home court?"

She folded her arms in front of her. "Of course, I'm making assumptions. I'm assuming that since you're one of only two local ministers, you're one person I should be talking to. Am I right? So tell me, what are you and your church doing to make these newcomers welcome?"

He stared at her. He didn't relish being put on the spot...but to be fair, no one ever enjoyed that. And

her point was valid. "You're right," he admitted.
She'd sized up the general situation accurately, but
nothing was ever…simple. There was always so much
to consider. Didn't she realize that? He cleared his
throat. "I *am* concerned and I *do* want to make the
newcomers welcome in Pleasant Prairie."

"Okay, so?" She looked up at him. It was an interesting pose. A historical biographer would have de-
scribed her expression as "looking at him askance."

He decided to give her a full answer. It was important that she didn't think that he hadn't done anything
constructive. "I've been doing a lot of reading about
American Hispanic culture and I've discussed with my
church's board the possibility of developing a community outreach with the newcomers in mind."

She rewarded him with a look of total disbelief.
"That's *all* you've done?"

Her tone belittled his effort, making it sound pa-
thetically inadequate. He clenched his jaw. "Yes."

"And just how long," she challenged him further,
"have the newcomers been here?"

The impression that he really didn't like Sophie's
cousin began to work its way through him—kind of a
slow burn. "They started moving in just after Christ-
mas—"

"So let me get this straight—" she cut him off
"—in the nearly six months since strangers arrived in
Pleasant Prairie, you've done some reading and dis-
cussing?" She arched one eyebrow at him.

The slow burn began roiling into a full boil. The

eyebrow really got him—it reminded him of a professor he hadn't liked in his undergraduate years. He stifled a rash response. As a pastor, he couldn't very well tell her to mind her own business. He took a measured breath. "In situations like this, I like to gather information and then formulate a plan—"

"And everyone is just supposed to wait around while you're gathering and formulating?" She raised her eyebrow a notch higher.

He felt his temperature rising higher. "I don't like going off half-cocked and putting peoples' backs up." Who did she think *she* was? Who did she think *he* was? "And besides, I'm not the mayor. I'm just a local pastor. I can develop programs at the church, but I can't make Pleasant Prairie or its people—"

She held up a hand, stopping him. "I don't think you're the mayor *or* that you can make people think or act the way you want them to." She paused and worried her lower lip.

He waited to see what outrageous thing she'd say next.

"But don't you see?" She pointed to the church. "You were sitting inside the church when these kids from the mobile home court were playing baseball right outside." Her look scorched him. "Why didn't you come out and try to, at least, talk to them, get to know them?"

That evening, Sophie's back door slammed, hard enough and loud enough to make Lucie jump in her chair on the front porch and wake up the little dog at her side that she'd decided to call Fella. She patted him reassuringly.

"Zoë! You come back here!" Sophie's harassed voice shrilled through the house. "You didn't finish cleaning the kitchen!"

"Got a date!" Zoë yelled. The old truck that the family used for hauling started with a roar, and within seconds, it barreled past Lucie, heading for the road to town.

Why was Zoë behaving so badly? Lucie folded the local paper she'd been reading and went inside to the kitchen. *Lord, it's just one thing after the other. I feel like I've slipped into quicksand. This house needs Your peace and healing—big-time!*

The little dog limped after her, no longer concerned about his awkward, one-stiff-legged gait. The baby mewling in her arms, Sophie stood in the middle of the kitchen. She had tears in her eyes.

Lord, Lucie prayed, *I see I'm needed here. Calm my heart. Give me peace so I can help Sophie.*

The kitchen still smelled of the ham they'd eaten and the scent of lemon dishwashing detergent. Lucie said nothing, just started cleaning the kitchen counters. Zoë had washed the supper dishes, leaving them in the drainer and dry side of the sink. But she had departed, leaving the rest of the job of cleaning the kitchen undone. Fella watched Lucie and then flopped down on the rug by the door. Lucie turned to her cousin. "Sit down and feed Carly. She sounds hungry."

Sophie didn't move.

Lucie pulled out a chair at the table and gently pushed her cousin into it. The baby began to wail in earnest and tugged at her mother's blouse. This got through to Sophie and she settled down to nurse the baby. For several minutes, the only sounds in the old house were the baby nursing hungrily—a kind of greedy smacking—and Lucie putting away dishes and silverware and running water to wipe the stove, table and counters.

"I love this kitchen." Sophie's voice was thick with unshed tears. "When I married Nate, he helped me strip the old wallpaper in here." She had a faraway look, and though her voice trembled, her expression looked wistful and happy. "We stripped and stripped—nine layers of wallpaper and a rainbow of different coats of paints in between."

"Wow." Lucie's voice sounded almost reverent in the evening stillness.

Sophie played with her daughter's dark curls. "This house is one hundred and twelve years old. Did you know that?" Sophie smiled, tears glistening in her eyes.

Finished, Lucie sat down in a chair, catercorner to Sophie and took her cousin's work-roughened hand. "Sophie, what's upsetting Zoë? She's at a constant boil. Did something happen? Or is this just because of Nate's accident?"

Sophie looked past Lucie's shoulder. "Nate stripped

all the cabinets and woodwork in the house for me, too. Because I loved the look of the natural wood.''

"Why is Zoë so angry and upset all the time?" Lucie pressed Sophie.

Her cousin ruffled Carly's waves. Tears dripped from her eyes. "What am I going to do, Lucie? They say Nate can't come home yet. He has to have intensive physical and occupational therapy. He might never be the same—" A sob cut off Sophie's words.

Lucie felt her heart constrict. *That bad? It's that bad, Lord?* In that instant, all her own plans for a summer of job-hunting disappeared. How could she leave Sophie to face this alone? *Oh, Lord, help me, help us.*

Mikey and Danny pounded up the back steps, shouting for their mommy. Fella moved awkwardly out of their way. Wiping away tears, Sophie stood up to meet her sons at the back door. But she asked in a voice just for Lucie, "Who will tend the crops Nate planted and bring in the harvest?"

In the late-morning sunshine of the next day, Lucie gazed at the garden plot, freshly plowed by a neighbor. Fella sat at her feet. When she'd reassured Sophie that she'd be happy to plant the kitchen garden, she hadn't realized that her concept of how large a garden should be clashed with her cousin's. Lucie's mother had always planted a vegetable or "kitchen" garden, a small plot of tomatoes, cucumbers, spinach, zucchini and leaf lettuce at the rear of the backyard. That was the size garden Lucie had been expecting.

But Sophie had become a farm wife. And her garden plot struck Lucie as the same size a Japanese farmer might call a farm!

Sophie sighed, sounding exhausted even after a full night's rest. "I bought tomato plants. About twenty."

Twenty tomato plants! We can't eat that many tomatoes!

"I can," Sophie said, answering Lucie's thoughts. "All our own tomato juice, sauce, salsa and spaghetti sauce."

"Really?" Lucie's already-low mood sank so deep, her toes tingled with it. Yesterday, she'd shelved her own summer plans. Sophie and Nate needed her.

But now this. Didn't Sophie dread the hours of labor she was so casually alluding to? In the past, Lucie had helped her mother—under duress—do some fall canning. Lucie knew the work was time-consuming, hot and uncomfortable. Feeling trapped, she realized that *she* would be the one helping Sophie do this canning.

Sweating in front of a hot stove while scalding skin off tomatoes was not Lucie's idea of time well spent. Canned vegetables were cheap enough at the grocery store. Didn't Sophie recall that Lucie wasn't known for her housewifely abilities? She could cook a meal if necessary. But only if necessary.

Sophie must have finally picked up on Lucie's unenthusiastic mien. "Are you sure you don't mind?"

Lucie forced a bright smile so she wouldn't make

Sophie feel guilty. "I've been looking forward to planting the garden." *Well, I had, Lord. Until I saw how big it is. You'll just have to multiply my original enthusiasm so it'll match the size of this humongous garden.*

"Where are the tomato plants?" Lucie asked with a show of bravado.

"The plants are in the shed behind the garage. You'll find garden gloves and all the tools there." Sophie walked away to the car. Mikey and Danny already waited in the nearby car. The boys would spend the day with friends on another farm while Lucie tackled the garden.

"Oh!" Sophie called over her shoulder. "Don't forget my kneeling pad. It's shaped like a watermelon slice. It'll save your knees!"

"Thanks. I'll use it." *You can bet your sweet life I will!*

Soon, Sophie was gone and Lucie was holding the pink rubber watermelon slice in one garden-gloved hand. Fella stiff-legged it over to the shade of a poplar tree and plumped down to watch her. Crows squawked overhead—probably making fun of her.

The hum of a vehicle coming up the road caused her to turn around. Who was it?

Chapter Three

In the gleaming sunlight, Tanner parked his car and got out. Shoving his hands into the back pockets of his jeans, he paused to take in the scene. Sophie's cousin, in cutoff shorts and with her golden curls ruffling in the wind, made an enticing picture. He longed to pause and enjoy the view and take another few moments to consider how to approach her. But Sophie's cousin was standing there, looking at him. And after yesterday's experience, he knew she wasn't the shy, quiet type. Plus she had zero patience.

He took a deep breath and approached her. *Lord, You know how this woman irritated me yesterday. Or I should say, her accusing me about not doing enough for the Hispanic newcomers got to me. But she's one of the few who has seen this community's need. This is need You laid on my heart soon after I came last year.*

His conscience added, *She also took action. Exactly what you've wanted to do, but haven't.*

This thought agitated inside him. But he had to discuss matters with her. Even if it was an unpleasant task, he needed her input. Yesterday, for the first time, he'd taken a small step toward connecting with the newcomers. And this morning, he'd had to admit that it had felt really good.

But now he faced one of the biggest challenges in his job as pastor—learning how to approach people and motivate them to volunteer in a way they would welcome, not resent. Case in point—this young woman, with her shapely legs and sassy mouth—had motivated him yesterday.

But he hadn't enjoyed it.

Lucie immediately recognized Tanner. *Oh, no! Not Mr. I'd-rather-be-reading-a-stuffy-book-than-playing baseball.* Reluctant to get into a prolonged conversation with him, she dropped the rubber watermelon slice and knelt on it. *Quick! Look busy.* From one of the pockets of the gardening apron she'd found in the shed and donned, she took a Popsicle stick, tied a string around it and jammed it into the tilled earth to begin to line up the garden rows.

With Fella barking his arrival, Tanner ambled up behind her. "Good morning."

His rich voice quivered through her. Glancing over her shoulder, she hushed the little dog. "Hi, Pastor." That was a good idea. *Keep it clear in your mind,*

Lucie. No matter how good-looking Tanner Bond is—this man is off-limits to you. He needs to find a nice little wife who wants to live in a small town in the middle of nowhere and wash his socks.

"Is Sophie already gone?"

Lucie pictured how he must look, long and lean in the morning sunshine. It was a dangerous exercise for her. "She's dropping the boys off at friends," she explained, fighting her awareness of him. "And then she's going to the hospital as usual."

"I see."

That's right. Sophie's not here so you can leave now. Beginning the planting, Lucie tore open the top of the green-bean seed envelope and poured the seeds into another pocket of the gardening apron. She slid the empty seed envelope onto the stick like a hat to mark the first row. When Tanner didn't make a move to leave, Lucie said, "She won't be back till late this afternoon. I'll tell her you called. Or you could find her at the hospital." *Well done, Lucie. Just the right touch of politeness combined with total unconcern.*

Tanner moved closer, right beside her.

Lucie's antenna quivered as he drew nearer. *You can stop right there, Pastor.*

"I visited Nate yesterday evening and saw Sophie then. I didn't come to see Sophie. Today I came to talk to you."

Keeping her eyes trained away from him, she was glad to hear that he was visiting Nate. It showed he was doing his duty, and that could only help her brother-in-law and Sophie.

But Tanner made her uncomfortable. *And why is that, Lucie?* her conscience prompted.

Yesterday, I was a bit brusque with him.

A bit brusque? her conscience chided her.

All right. I was rude. She sighed. One of her shortcomings was impatience. But if he'd come to see her, why didn't he just say why he did? She quelled the impatience she was feeling and asked in a measured tone, "What can I do for you?"

"About that baseball game yesterday—"

"I apologize." She felt herself color warmly. "I didn't mean to speak so…abruptly. It was an upsetting day…." Once started, her alibis just kept coming. "I mean injuring the dog, getting the bum's rush at Shangri-La Estates—"

"I understand." He sounded as if he did.

A heavy, waiting silence hung over them. She heard him shifting his feet and again, steeled herself against turning toward him. She couldn't afford to look up at his chiseled features or the sympathetic expression she imagined he'd have. That would be a killer combination.

He cleared his throat again. "You were right. I shouldn't have been sitting inside the church while those kids were playing ball just a stone's throw away. I want St. Andrew's to be the kind of church that has an open door to its community. I'd like the kids—

anyone—to feel comfortable about dropping in if they need something…." His voice trailed off.

She listened, suddenly liking Tanner Bond a whole lot more than she had just minutes before. "So?" she prompted.

"This is my first pastorate," he said in a humble voice. "I'm still trying to get that atmosphere started."

It had cost Tanner Bond a lot to say that. It would cost any man to admit that he was still green. Impressed, Lucie stood up and turned sideways to face him.

Facing him cost her, too. Why did she have to keep noticing things about him? Like the flecks of gold in his brown irises?

Glancing away, down at the dark earth around her feet, she wondered what she could do to help this man. At the same time, she realized something about the chore she was doing. Before she started planting, she needed to string all the rows first. Otherwise, her seeded rows could turn out crooked like a crazy quilt. And stringing the rows all by herself would take forever.

She propped a hand on each hip. Working together would give them something to do while talking, a good way to take her mind off the man himself. And it would make the conversation easier for both of them, a lesson she'd learned from watching her own dad, also a pastor.

She held out the end of the string to Tanner. "Why don't you help me with this? If you hold the end of the string for me, it will help me get the rows straight.''

He looked down at the end of the ball of string she was offering him as if he had difficulty getting what she wanted him to do. Then he reached out and took the string. His hand brushed hers enticingly.

Her skin tingled. Why did he have to be so good-looking? He just stood there—every woman's dream! Why couldn't he wear thick glasses or have a cowlick that stuck up in his hair? Why was he able to get to her? Was it because he cared?

His openness and sincerity touched her. And he had taken action when push came to shove. He had joined in the impromptu softball game yesterday and made the kids happy.

''You want me opposite you, right?'' His voice brought her back to task.

Without more ado, he unrolled the string from the ball she held. He tugged on it till he stood across from her, the width of the garden plot. He made a show of sighting down the string to be sure it was straight. ''How's this?''

''Fine.'' She swallowed trying to moisten her mouth. ''Fine,'' she croaked. He pulled a pocketknife out, cut the string and then looked at her expectantly. She hurried to him and gave him a handful of sticks and took the ball of the string from him and drew it to the other end to start the next row.

The ironic symbolism of the string attaching her to him wasn't lost on her. *No strings attached, please.*

"What…" She cleared her throat. "What exactly did you want me to help you with?" *Let's get right to the point and get this over with.*

Her curiosity expanding like yeast dough on a warm stove, she waited. They continued to work together silently, stringing row after row.

As they worked, he appeared to be deep in thought. Lucie waited and waited. Finally she met him at the end of another row. "You've stalled long enough. Come on. Tell me."

He frowned. "Yesterday, you sized up the sticky situation at the mobile home court pretty well."

"Yes." Wanting to hurry this oh-so-deliberate man along, she let him know she was up to speed on this topic. "Sophie tells me that the packing plant outside of town brought up the Mexican-Americans from south Texas to take the jobs no one else wanted."

He nodded. "That's right."

"She said some people around here weren't too happy about it." Lucie paused and gave him a significant glance.

"I think it's more because around here people aren't used to strangers moving in—"

"So?" Lucie prompted. She walked away from him, drawing the string with her, aware that his intense gaze followed her every move.

"I noticed you spoke some Spanish the other day," he said.

"I minored in Spanish, but my degree is in art education." *Please get to the point, Tanner. What do you want? Me to translate for you?* "But if the people at the mobile home park are Mexican-Americans from Texas, they can speak English. You don't need an interpreter."

"That woman and the children at the mobile home park didn't speak English to you—not willingly, did they?" he countered, raising an eyebrow at her.

Ignoring how appealing this expression was on him, she bent down and poked another stick in the warming earth. "You don't need an interpreter," she reiterated. *You don't need me, Pastor.*

He ignored her objection. "I've gone to the park and knocked on doors, inviting them to church and the children to Sunday school, but all I get is *'No hablo inglés.'*"

"Maybe they don't feel welcome. That Go Home Mexicans painted over the Shangri-La sign can't have helped…community relations."

"I know. And at the high school, there was trouble at the end of the school year." He frowned as he unwound more string across from her. "Fighting. Name-calling."

I have to give him big points for being so concerned about this. Softening, she glanced over at him and then bent to plant another stick. "What do you plan to do to change it?"

"That's what I came to ask your help with." He gazed at her, dubious hope in his eyes. "What do you think we should do?"

We? She stared back at him. He'd asked for her

help, but she doubted he'd be up to it. "Was yesterday the first time those kids came to play ball?"

He frowned. "I think so. Though I can't say absolutely—"

What he needed to do was so obvious. Why couldn't he see it? She grinned at him. He wouldn't relish her next suggestion. "Then why don't we—I mean *you*—invite them back?" she proposed. "If they knew they'd have a pitcher, maybe they'd start coming daily. It would give you a chance to get to know—"

Tanner raised a hand to halt her. "I—"

"Hey!" Slamming the back door after her, Zoë, wearing her white DQ shirt and black shorts, ran down the steps toward Lucie. "You let me oversleep! I'm supposed to open the DQ today! I gotta be there in ten minutes!"

The girl's aggrieved tone and stormy expression put Lucie's teeth on edge. Hoping she wasn't betraying this, she turned to the girl. "Sophie said you didn't work till after—"

Zoë gave a huff of impatience. "Sophie can't keep my schedule straight. I gotta go."

"So what's stopping you?" Lucie asked without sympathy. She sensed Tanner bristling at Zoë's attitude.

"Just because I was in a little after curfew last night, Sophie took my keys to the truck away—*again*. That means you gotta take me in—*again*." Zoë glared at Lucie.

Lucie didn't believe in hitting children, but for just

a moment, she understood why a parent might be tempted to threaten to "slap that expression off your face."

Tanner spoke up. "Zoë, the youth group is planning a trip to—"

Lucie was surprised by his intervening. *Way to go, Tanner. Hang in there.*

"I heard all about the trip to Des Moines and Adventureland," Zoë cut him off. "I'm not interested in kid stuff. I gotta go now or I'll be late for work! And jobs don't grow on trees around this Podunk burg."

Tanner motioned Zoë to his car. "Lucie, you've got enough to handle here. I'll run her in for you." He walked away. "Go ahead and start planting the rows we've strung. I have to take care of something in town and then I'll be back out to help you string the rest."

"That's all right," Lucie said, not really wanting him to return. "You don't—"

"I'll be back in a half hour!"

Lucie recognized defeat and felt grumpy about it. Zoë's behavior was dreadful. But foremost in her mind was Tanner.

His approach to the problem of integrating the newcomers into Pleasant Prairie was to knock on their doors and invite them to church and Sunday school? That must have gone over like a ton of bricks. He didn't look clueless, but he obviously needed help in the area of people skills. And he'd come to her, the last person in Pleasant Prairie who wanted to work with him.

She watched him drive away.

Why me, Lord? Sophie and the kids need me. I'm planting a garden the size of Wyoming. Zoë's a disaster waiting to happen. Who knows what she'll get into this summer?

And now Tanner wants me to get him started with a problem like this? The man doesn't have a clue of how to go about it. And what about me? I need a job! I'm broke. Isn't there anyone else to help Tanner? I'm not a superhero!

Later, the wall phone rang in Sophie's kitchen just as Lucie and Fella walked in. Lucie picked up the receiver.

"Hello, Lucie?"

Instantly recognizing the pleasant soft voice on the phone, Lucie slid onto the wooden kitchen chair. She'd finally come in to have a late lunch. The garden was only half-planted. Mirroring her fatigue, Fella slumped beside her feet, panting. She patted his head affectionately and took a deep breath. "Hi, Mom."

"How's Sophie, dear?"

Lucie cut right to the chase. "I won't be back home for the foreseeable future."

"I was afraid of that." Concern vibrated in her mother's voice. "Should I come?"

"I can handle it." Lucie tried to keep the hopelessness out of her voice. But didn't her poor mother, the pastor's wife, have enough to handle with her endless round of church meetings and volunteering? Lucie wouldn't add another burden.

"What about your job hunt?" Her mother's voice was hesitant.

Hearing her worry put into words pinched Lucie. "That will have to wait." The gruff words scraped her throat.

"I'm sorry, dear. But God can handle that. How are you doing for money? Should Dad and I send you—"

"Mom, I'm okay," she nearly snapped. She didn't want to ask her parents for money. *I should be past those days by now.*

From his place at her feet, Fella yipped for his lunch.

"Just a minute, Fella," Lucie crooned, glad of distraction.

"Did Sophie get a dog for the boys?" her mother asked.

"No, I'm responsible for Fella being here *and* with a cast on his leg." Now Lucie felt the need of her mother's always-ready sympathy. "Mom, I feel terrible. He ran in front of the Bomb and I clipped him."

"Oh, honey, I'm so sorry."

"It wasn't too bad, I guess. Just a broken leg. The vet said the accident could easily have been fatal. But I'm having trouble finding Fella's owner." She hurried to explain. "The vet thinks he belongs to a family in the trailer court just outside of town. But when I checked, I didn't have any luck finding them."

"Well, let Fella find them for you. He'll know his own door."

Her mother's common sense wowed Lucie. "You're right! Thanks, Mom."

Her mother chuckled. "Call us if you need anything, dear. I have to go now. I'm late to my first meeting of the day—the young mother's club."

After their farewells, Lucie walked over and opened a can of dog food. "Here you go, Fella. I think my mom has solved your problem."

As she bent to empty the can into Fella's dish, she thought again of her mother and her endless round of church-related activities. *Poor Mom. What a life. The church should pay her a salary, too.*

The phone rang again. Lucie lifted the receiver. "Hi, Lucie here."

"Lucie?" Tanner's voice greeted her. "Sorry I didn't get back to help you with the rest of the garden. A workman showed up at the church to put in a new electrical circuit board."

"No problem. It's planted." *Almost.* "I'm just about to put supper in the Crock-Pot to slow cook. Sophie and the boys will be hungry when they hit the door."

"I still want to get together with you to talk more—"

An idea snapped in Lucie's mind. She'd kill two birds with one stone and not be forced into a tête-à-tête with this handsome, young minister. "Great. I'll pick you up. You can go with me to Shangri-La after supper tonight—''

"I—"

"Can't talk now," she cut him off. "I'll pick you up in front of the church at seven."

She hung up and looked down at Fella, who was eating enthusiastically. "Well, he might as well know how I operate. I'm not going to sit around talking about what to do. He's done that for more than six months. It's time for action. And if Tanner Bond can't get stand the heat, he better get out of the kitchen. I'm not my mother, the meek and mild pastor's wife."

Fella looked up at her as though making a comment.

"Yes, I know I don't have time for all this extra stuff. But evidently, I *am* my father's daughter. I can't see a need in a community and just walk away. Darn."

At seven in front of St. Andrew's bright red double doors, Tanner looked disgruntled as he got into the Bomb. "We could take my car," he muttered.

Lucie had predicted he'd say this. Why did men always think they had to be in the driver's seat? "The Bomb has made it this far," she replied airily. "It should get us all the way to Shangri-La." She drove through town, the young pastor beside her, and turned heads. With an insouciant grin, Lucie waved and people looked away circumspectly.

Oops! I forgot about small-town gossip. And Tanner's the pastor, the young eligible pastor. They'll have us engaged by morning. I should have just met

*him at the mobile home court. Please, Lord, don't let
this touch off the local rumor mill.*

As they headed toward Shangri-La, Lucie decided
she needed more information. "So tell me more about
how the community has been handling the Hispanic
newcomers?" When he didn't answer right away, she
glanced at him. He was frowning. *Still holding back?*
"Come on."

He grimaced. "Are you always so…outspoken?"

"Yes," she said. "Now spill it." She didn't have
any patience for his weighing and measuring every
word. It just wasted time.

"What are you planning tonight?" he asked in a
wary tone.

"I asked first," she reminded him, her voice tight.

He grunted his disapproval, but answered, "All
right. They're convenient targets for everything that
happens."

"Such as?" *Is he going to make me drag every bit
out of him?*

"Kids have been stealing trucks off farms. You
know how everyone just leaves the keys in vehicles
around here."

She nodded, aware that farmers had so many ma-
chines and vehicles and they didn't want to be bothered carrying rings of keys. And in the past, they
hadn't had to worry about vehicles being stolen. How
could anyone make a fast getaway with a tractor?

"Anyway, I think it's just some kids joyriding. The
trucks are always found abandoned in the area."

"But some people are saying it's the newcomers?"

"Yes, but there isn't any proof that it is. It's just easier to suspect a stranger." He sounded indignant.

She liked him for that. She hated injustice, too.

She drove through the entrance of the mobile home court. "But nothing specific? No situation where a Hispanic was caught doing something?"

"Well, one Mexican-American teen was caught trying to let some cattle out of a pasture. Unfortunately, it was a farm right on the highway. It could have caused an accident, injuring cattle and motorists."

"Not good." With twilight glowing around them in the soft late-spring air, she parked in the visitor's parking area and got out. She opened the back door and urged Fella off the seat by tugging on his new leash.

"Why did you bring the dog?" He stared at her distrustfully. "And now it's my turn for an answer. What exactly have you got up your sleeve?"

"First, I still think that Fella belongs to someone here. And my mom suggested that a dog would know which door is his."

Tanner looked impressed. "Good idea. Your mother has her wits about her."

Her wits about her? The man talks like a book.

"Okay. What's second on your agenda?" he persisted.

Fella looked around and then began sniffing the air.

"Okay," she gave in. "About getting the Mexican-Americans and the locals together—the baseball game in the park yesterday morning seems to me to be a good place for us to start—''

Suddenly Fella took off, his casted leg barely slowing him in his rush. It was all Lucie could do to keep up with him and hang on to the leash.

With Tanner at her side, Lucie raced after the dog. ''Slow down, Fella! You might hurt your leg!''

After a short run down the first lane, Fella charged up the steps of a dusty trailer. Fella barked excitedly. But no one came to the door.

Lucie shortened Fella's leash and knocked on the door. From behind her on the step, she could feel Tanner's hesitance. She ignored it.

The door opened finally. A short, stocky Latino man frowned at her.

Fella leaped up, barking in a frenzy of joy.

Afraid the dog might hurt himself in his excitement, Lucie bent down and picked him up. He wriggled in her arms, trying to break away and leap inside.

''Whatever you're sellin', we don't want it.'' Ignoring Fella, the man started to close the door.

''Wait!'' Lucie edged forward. ''I'm trying to find this dog's owner—''

''I don't know the dog. I never seen it before.'' The man tugged on the doorknob.

''Then why did he lead us right to this door?'' Lucie asked.

''I don't know,'' the man said with obvious irritation.

"Are you sure he's not yours?" Tanner interposed. "We're just trying to help."

"No, and I'm gonna shut this door *now*." And he did.

Fella struggled in her arms. Lucie stumbled against Tanner and he caught her before she lost her balance. Fella barked frantically, nearly leaping from her arms.

With a firm hand, Tanner took hold of her elbow and led her down the metal steps. Then he walked her away at a brisk pace.

She ignored the barking dog and Tanner. What was going on here? Fella obviously knew the man, obviously wanted to get inside. Suddenly she pulled away from Tanner and turned back toward the trailer.

"What?" Tanner expostulated.

Or that's how he sounded to her. She liked that old-fashioned word *expostulated*. It fit the sound he made, a sound of objection, of wanting to hold her back. And though she appreciated his concern and having him with her, it didn't work. Expostulation or not, she had to try again.

With Tanner right beside her, grimacing with disapproval, she went back and knocked on the same door.

Still in her arms, Fella began barking again, though he sounded heartbroken now. The dejected sound made her feel even more sorry for the little dog.

The man's voice came through the open window. "Who is it?"

"It's me, Lucie Hansen," she shouted over Fella's

barking. "This is obviously your dog. I'm really sorry about hitting him. It was an accident. But I've paid the vet. All I want to do is return him to his owner. I can't keep him—"

The door opened a crack.

"Sammie," the man bellowed, "get away from that door!"

"But, Papa—"

The sight of the child electrified the dog. Wild now, Fella almost succeeded in leaping from her arms. That sealed it in Lucie's mind. *This is your home, Fella.*

"*¡Cierra la puerta!*" the man roared. "Shut it!"

The door slammed. "Go away, lady!" the man yelled. He added a loud string of insults in Spanish for good measure.

Tanner pushed forward. "There's no need to be rude," he shouted back, unexpectedly. "She's just trying to do a good deed. You ought to be thanking her. And on second thought, I wouldn't leave a dog with someone like you—"

"Tanner," she cautioned him. This time she drew him away with her. She took him by the elbow and tugged him down the first step. Tanner allowed this, but he kept casting heated glances back at the trailer.

From her arms, Fella looked over her shoulder at the receding trailer, yipping. It was a painful sound to hear. She stroked the dog's ruffled fur. By the time they reached her car, Fella had quieted. But he still whimpered on and off. It broke her heart. *Sorry, Fella. I don't understand why they didn't want you, either.*

"Well, we didn't accomplish much with that," Tanner said close to her ear, sounding sympathetic. He looked down at her, concern for her in his expression. "Don't let it upset you. That man just doesn't want his son's dog back."

She opened the back door and gently settled Fella, who was panting heavily, on the back seat, on the towel spread there. She then shut the door and leaned back against the Bomb. "I don't know if we accomplished anything. I'm sure Fella knew that trailer. And that little boy—"

Tanner opened the driver's side door for her. "You can't make him take responsibility for the dog if he doesn't want to." Tanner took a deep breath. "Let's go back to town. I'll buy you a cup of coffee at the café and we'll discuss this. I want—"

Her mind busy sorting out what had just taken place, she heard him only from a distance. "Not yet," she said simply, and looked around. Had they been observed?

Of course, people had peeped out their windows. They'd watched Tanner, Fella and her. She and Tanner might as well take advantage of it. *This trip is not going to be wasted! I'm not leaving without getting something started.*

"What?" Tanner objected.

She pursed her lips, looking up at him, letting him see that she was undeterred. "Let's knock on a few more doors."

"What?"

"You're starting to repeat yourself." She shrugged. "I don't know about you, but I don't give up that easily. I'm here.. *I'm* going to do something besides just talk."

Lucie saw that her words had stung him, but she couldn't think about his ruffled feathers. Besides, Tanner had come to *her* looking for help. Not vice versa.

"While Sophie takes little Carly to sit with Nate again tomorrow," she went on, "I'll have Mikey and Danny again for the day. Why can't we spend the morning at the ball diamond in the park? At the very least, we'll get to know some of the kids here. It would be a start—"

He tried to interrupt.

"Now, we're just going to knock on a few doors," she said in a soothing voice, "and talk about baseball practice tomorrow." She heard Tanner grind his teeth.

"I don't like to do things on the spur of the moment," he said in an exasperated undertone. "We haven't had a chance to talk this through—"

"What's to talk about?" Through the car window, she told Fella to stay, she'd be back soon. "We're going to invite kids to come to the park for a softball practice tomorrow morning. What trouble could that stir up?" She started away. "Think of it as a kind of a community survey."

He tried to catch her arm and stop her.

She marched up the steps of the next trailer,

Chapter Four

Tanner couldn't believe his eyes. Lucie headed back toward the trailers. He started after her. Someone had to keep her from stepping over the line. Didn't she realize her impulsiveness could stir up real trouble?

Lord, this woman is going to drive me crazy! This morning, we just talked for a few minutes—make that seconds—about doing something. I haven't even had time to pray about it—

Already up the nearest set of steps, Lucie knocked on the metal door, which was painted glossy turquoise. The woman who opened the door eyed Lucie with a worried expression.

Tanner stiffened, ready to defend Lucie against more verbal abuse.

Seemingly oblivious to the woman's wary expression, Lucie beamed at her. "Hello, I'm—"

"I don't want no trouble," the woman interrupted.

"This isn't about trouble," Lucie went on cheerily. "I was at the city park yesterday and played softball with some children I think live here—"

"Why shouldn't they play at the park? We live here," the woman blustered, her face coloring.

"I'm glad they were there," Lucie continued without missing a beat. "They let my nephews Mikey and Danny join in. We had a great time. I was just wondering if you knew any of the children—littler ones, elementary school kids—who might want to play another game there tomorrow morning?"

Tanner waited for the woman's response. When it came, it surprised him.

"Don't you work for a living?" the woman asked, looking wary.

Lucie chuckled. "I wish. But I'm here helping my cousin Sophie this summer. Her husband was hurt in an accident and is laid up in the hospital. So I'll be bringing her boys to the park every day." Lucie again beamed at the woman.

The amount of personal information Lucie willingly revealed to a total stranger amazed Tanner. But it worked. Lucie's easygoing, friendly way had plainly softened the woman.

And that drained away his anger at Lucie's impetuousness. Maybe softball in the park would open an opportunity to reach out to the newcomers. Maybe he'd underestimated Lucie.

"That your man?" The woman nodded toward him.

Lucie laughed.

The sound surged through Tanner, awakening a new awareness of this petite live wire next to him. He clamped down on his reaction, not letting it leak into his expression. But to his chagrin, he couldn't stop his neck from warming at the woman's question.

"No, this is the pastor of the church next to the park." Lucie grinned, no doubt enjoying his embarrassment. "He was playing ball with the kids, too."

"Hello," Tanner said, feeling and sounding awkward.

"Padre," the woman responded with a polite nod.

He nodded back, wishing he could talk to a stranger as effortlessly as Lucie did.

"So," Lucie coaxed, "do you have any kids or know any who would like to meet in the park for a little baseball?"

"Try next door," the woman said, and closed the door.

Off Lucie trotted, down the steps and up to the next door. On the other side of the lane, little children with skinned knees and solemn eyes had gathered, staring at them.

Tanner wished he could at least slow Lucie down, but gave up. Might as well try to hold back a tidal wave.

At the second door, Lucie repeated the performance—affable, unfazed by the almost identical hostility she met. She invited the mother to tell her kids that they'd be in the park tomorrow morning ready to pitch the ball for any kids wanting to play.

How did she do it? Talk to strangers without the least qualm? She baffled and impressed Tanner in spite of himself.

"Hey!" a familiar voice hailed Lucie from the lane. "Hey! Señorita Lucie!"

Tanner looked around and saw the cocky kid from the ball game, riding up on a bike. What was his name?

"Miguel!" Lucie waved at the youngster. "*¡Hola!* Good to see you."

Miguel halted by them, straddling his battered, slightly too-big bike. "What you doin' here, *señorita?*"

"I was looking for you." Lucie smiled. "Mikey and Danny and I are going to be in the park tomorrow morning around ten. Want to play some ball?"

Miguel looked past her to Tanner. "You brought *him* with you?"

Lucie chuckled again. "Yes, I decided he should be allowed out of the church for good behavior. He helped me plant a garden this morning."

Tanner felt steam rising through him. She didn't need to emphasize how inept he felt in this situation.

"Okay," Miguel conceded. "You gonna to pitch to us again?"

"I'll be there. Bring your friends," Lucie invited.

"Okay." Miguel rose up on his pedals again. "See you tomorrow!" He rode away down the curved lane of ill-kept grass and dandelions.

Lucie turned to Tanner. "That was lucky. We'll just

knock on a few more doors and then we can go. Miguel will spread the word.''

Tanner had a lot he wanted to say to her, but he limited himself to ''I think we ought to leave. We need to talk this all over. Plunging into things headlong can cause unexpected complications….'' When he realized he was just talking to himself, he stopped. Lucie had already mounted the next black metal staircase.

Fuming, Tanner hurried after her and ran up the steps behind her. ''Lucie—''

''This time,'' she said in an undertone, ''you do the talking.'' Then she took a step back, leaving him in the forefront—just as the door opened.

Tanner found himself confronting a large Latino man.

''Yeah?'' the man barked.

No time for objections or hesitation. Tanner cleared his throat. ''Good evening.'' Tanner's mind raced. *Just act natural, like Lucie.* He offered the man his hand. ''I'm the pastor at the church next to the town park. We're here inviting children to softball practice at the diamond tomorrow morning.''

The man reluctantly shook his hand. ''Why? You people don't want us in your town or your park.''

Tanner felt himself sweating around his collar and it wasn't from the warm evening. ''That may have been the impression you have gotten. But St. Andrew's is glad you're here. Do you have any children who'd be interested in softball practice?''

The man looked him over, from head to toe. "I'll think about it."

Relief flowed through Tanner.

"*Gracias,*" Lucie said. "We'll look forward to it. *¡Adiós!*"

Tanner followed her down to the lane again. Lucie had pushed him to do what he most dreaded, trying to connect with these strangers and take some positive action. Achieving his goal left him with a weird mixture of reactions, one of which was the desire to kick up his heels. The other was to hug Lucie. He suppressed both.

"I think we can go now." Lucie headed off for her car.

But Tanner caught up with her. She'd taken the lead all evening, but now he would get his word in. They'd been lucky—blessed—but they needed to plan and ask God for guidance. "We are going to go somewhere and talk about this—*now.*"

She had the nerve to laugh. "Okay. How about the DQ? I have to pick up Zoë anyway. You can treat me to a fudge brownie sundae."

"I'm driving," he declared. His tone must have convinced her because she let him usher her to the passenger side. He opened the door. She brushed past him—so close. He ignored the temptation to trace the enticing softness of her cheek.

Forcing his mind back to the mundane task of driving, he got in the other side and started the car. The muffler roared. "You need to get that fixed," he commented, "before it drops off."

"I'm a little short on cash…right now."

He recalled that she'd replied to the woman's question "Don't you work for a living?" with "I wish." He remembered how short cash had been when he'd finished his bachelor's degree, too. *I'll have to find her a way to make some spending money while she helps out Sophie and Nate.*

Listening to her pleasant chatter to Fella, he drove toward the nearby trailer court exit. Lucie's vivacity blossomed in the car, lightening Tanner's mood in spite of himself.

A man with dark, weathered skin and long silver hair stood very straight beside the lane just inside the trailer court exit. He flagged them down. Through Tanner's open window, he said with an engaging smile, "My car is fixed in town. I need a ride to the garage. Can you take me?"

Tanner glanced to Lucie. They were in Pleasant Prairie and the man looked safe enough, but she owned the car, after all.

She nodded. "Sure. Get in the back. That's Fella on the seat."

The older man went around to the door behind Lucie's and got in. "*Gracias.* Thank you. You know the garage?"

"Sure. There's only one in town." Tanner drove out of the trailer park and turned toward town. He hoped having another person in the car would dilute

Lucie's effervescent effect on him. He couldn't let her charm him away from a serious discussion. *It's my turn now, Lucie. And you're going to listen.*

"So you named Pepe 'Fella'?" the older man commented, patting the dog's head.

"Pepe?" Lucie asked, an edge of excitement in her voice. "You know this dog?"

Tanner echoed her silently.

"Yes. I'm Ignacio Valdez." Over the top of the seat, he offered a hand to Lucie. "I overheard your conversation about the dog."

"I'm Lucie Hansen. And this is Tanner Bond, the pastor—"

"At St. Andrew's," Ignacio finished for her. "Good evening, *padre*."

"Same to you, Mr. Valdez," Tanner replied, wondering when this man had connected him with the church. Tonight or earlier? Tanner was certain he'd have noticed Valdez's long silver hair in the midst of his crew-cut and feed-cap congregation.

"Call me Ignacio. I'm not a formal man."

Before Tanner could answer him, Lucie chimed in again, "Do you know who Fella—I mean Pepe—belongs to?"

In the rearview mirror, Tanner saw Ignacio nodding.

"You took him to his door. Or he took you? That was a quite a race." The older man grinned. "Little Sammie Torres had only snuck Pepe in a week ago."

"But the man at the door," Tanner put in, "said Fella didn't belong—"

"Sammie's father, Big Sam, never liked the dog. I think he may have taken Pepe and dropped him back on the highway."

"That's awful," Lucie moaned.

Lucie's genuine distress touched Tanner. Her abundant sympathy and caring loosened something deep inside him.

Ignacio shrugged. "It's a small trailer. Sam could lose his job at the packing plant at any time. It's a long drive back to south Texas. Hard on a dog. Hard to make a boy leave a dog behind."

Tanner mulled this over. As he recalled the scene at the Torres's door, he recalled the fatigue in the man's voice and face. *A rough life.* So different from his own.

Lucie, of course, was the kind who jumped to conclusions. Her sympathy would be with the little boy and dog. And though Tanner hadn't liked the way Sam Torres had behaved, the people who lived at the mobile home court hadn't come to Pleasant Prairie because of the scenery.

They'd needed jobs badly enough to drive thousands of miles to get them. And those jobs were the ones Iowans didn't want anymore—hard jobs where they stood long hours and got their hands dirty. He needed to impress on her that she couldn't see this situation with Fella as just black and white.

"I heard you are starting a morning baseball practice," Ignacio commented conversationally. "I myself played *beisbol* for a farm team in Texas when I was

a young man. What a way to make a few bucks.''
Ignacio shook his head, smiling. "*Fue muy divertido.
It was fun.*"

The older man's words made Lucie's heart beat faster. They were like an answer to prayer. She glanced
sideways at Tanner. Looking deep in thought, he drove
into the outskirts of town. Had he heard that? Would
he let an opening like this pass him by?

"That's really interesting, isn't it, Tanner?'' She
dug a fingernail into his firm side.

Stirred from his thoughts, he winced and turned to
her. "Sure.''

Clueless. The man needed her. She groaned silently.
I don't want to be needed. But the memory of his
quick defense of her at the Torres's door flashed in
her mind, warming her.

She half turned to look into the older man's lined
face. "Could we interest you in stopping by the ball
field tomorrow morning about ten? Tanner and I will
be there to pitch the ball and coach a little.''

Ignacio grinned, but didn't reply.

Tanner drove up to the fifties-vintage cement-block
building that housed Mitch's Garage.

Ignacio opened the car door. "*¡Amigo!*" he hailed,
"Mitch! I'm here, ready to pay!''

The mechanic, reaching up to pull down the wide
garage door to close up, halted. "Hey, *amigo* yourself,
I'd just about given up on you.''

"My daughter couldn't bring me, so I finally caught
a ride with these folks.'' Ignacio gave Fella a parting

pat on the head and got out of the Bomb. *"Gracias. Muchas gracias* for the ride."

"Don't mention it," Lucie replied.

Mitch looked at Lucie. "This your car?"

Lucie nodded.

"You need to bring it in for an estimate on a new muffler," the mechanic said.

Lucie shrugged. *Why get an estimate before I can afford the muffler? Lord, I'd appreciate that part-time job sooner rather than later, please!*

"The way it sounds you don't have much longer on this one," Mitch warned.

Unfortunately, Lucie had to agree with him as Tanner put the noisy car into Reverse.

As the car edged backward, Lucie leaned out the window and called, "See you tomorrow, Ignacio!"

The silver-haired man waved, but gave her no promise.

Tanner drove west toward the DQ at the other end of town. The deepening dusk highlighted his chiseled profile. Sunk in thought, he didn't even turn to look at her.

She wondered uneasily if he was upset with her. But that's what she wanted, wasn't it? Well, not exactly. She just wanted him not to be really comfortable with her. And especially not depending on her. *I'll help you get started, Tanner. Then I'm out of it.*

"I didn't have time to make myself something to eat," he said as he pulled into the DQ parking lot, "so I'm going to order a burger. What do you want?"

He didn't sound displeased with her. But maybe he was just good at masking his emotions. He seemed like the type, or was it because he'd learned this was the best way for a clergyman? How did people do that, anyway? She'd never even tried to hide her emotions, much to her mother's dismay.

Lucie scanned the scene. It was DQ season, all right. Cars and trucks filled the lot. Teens sat in cars, playing their music and calling to one another. Lucie noticed an invisible, but very real, dividing line between the Hispanic teens and the homegrown ones.

"What do you want?" Tanner repeated. "Can you really eat a whole fudge brownie sundae? They're huge."

She brought her mind back to him. "Yes, and I want extra whipped cream. I worked up an appetite." She looked over her shoulder. "And a dish of vanilla for Fella. He's looks like the vanilla type, don't you think?" she teased.

Coming around, Tanner opened the car door for her. He gazed down at her as if he were trying to classify her as animal, vegetable or mineral.

"Lighten up, Bond," she purred, and hopped out of the car. "A little soft serve won't hurt Fella. And he deserves a treat." She watched for Tanner's reaction.

"Whatever." Declining her challenge, he closed the door and escorted her to the ordering window.

Another battered and dusty truck of teens screeched into the lot. Teens sat in the cab and in the bed. Wasn't riding in the truck bed against the law? It certainly wasn't safe.

At the order window, Zoë slouched, looking through the screen with the slider panel.

"Hi, Zoë," Lucie said in a restrained voice, hoping the girl wouldn't be rude in public.

"You're early," the girl snapped. "I got another half hour."

Lucie didn't make any response to Zoë's impolite greeting. Someone needed to do something about that girl. But not Lucie. *Maybe Mom should come for a visit.*

Tanner pulled out his billfold. "I'll take a burger, fries, root beer, a fudge brownie sundae and a dish of vanilla."

In the midst of scribbling this on a notepad, Zoë glanced past Lucie. One look at the local guys jumping out of the just-arrived truck and Zoë underwent a transformation. She slouched, but now more artistically, like she had a part in a music video. And a grin she tried hard to hide lifted her face.

This was the first grin Lucie had seen on Zoë's face since she'd arrived in Pleasant Prairie. Uneasy now, Lucie watched, wanting to identify which one of the guys had lit Zoë's lightbulb.

Trying to hide her excitement, Zoë looked down as she took Tanner's money, put it in the register and gave him his order number. Tanner and Lucie stepped aside from the window.

"Hey! Zoë!" The leader of the pack called out as he strutted toward her.

"Hi, Riel," Zoë returned, looking down at her order pad.

With straight dark hair and green eyes, Riel wore the country western chic so popular in rural areas, and also sported an earring and a serpent tattoo on his arm.

Lucie's gut told her that instead of the snake, *TROUBLE—BIG TIME* should have been tattooed on his forehead. She groaned inwardly. Did Sophie know about Riel? Lucie kept her expression carefully nonchalant, though her stomach did an uncomfortable jig.

Tanner and she stepped farther away as Riel and friends crowded around, putting in their orders.

Lucie listened to Zoë giggle at Riel's cool chatter and felt at least a zillion years older than the teen.

When Zoë called Tanner's number, the teens fell back at his approach. He picked up a fragrant white bag and the ice cream from the window and walked Lucie over to the car again.

She got in and took the ice cream from him. His expression revealed little of what was going on inside his head. That bothered her. But why?

Reaching over the back seat, Lucie set the dish of ice cream in front of Fella and then turned back, dipping her red plastic spoon into the hot fudge. "Do you know who that Riel is?" she asked Tanner.

"What?" he asked, still clueless.

Fleetingly, Lucie recalled a TV talk show she'd seen, featuring an author who'd written a book about males and females coming from different planets. Was Tanner Bond even on the same planet as she was right now?

"When we were at the window," she asked, "did you recognize any of the kids who came up behind us?"

"No. Why?"

She shook her head at him. "*Because* Zoë looked like she was interested in that kid she called Riel."

"You shouldn't jump to conclusions," Tanner said, and then bit a fry in two.

"And you're a turtle in human form," she replied without missing a beat. She stole one of his fries. "Stick your head out of that shell and see what's going on."

To their far left, a young Mexican-American male got out of a beat-up station wagon and escorted his girlfriend toward the window. Several of his friends trailed behind him.

"At least I don't *push* people," Tanner said. "Going back to Torres's door when he'd told you plainly that he didn't want to be bothered was a mistake." He sank his teeth into his burger and catsup dripped down his chin. He wiped it off with a white paper napkin.

Still tracking the scene in front of them, she worried her lower lip. "Maybe, but I had to try. Maybe my…persistence will make him reconsider. Besides—" she cocked an eyebrow at Tanner "—you got a little heated with Torres yourself."

He reddened. "I didn't like the way he was talking

to you—even if you had stepped over the line.'' His voice roughened.

She made eye contact with him. "Why didn't you tune in on the fact that Ignacio let us know that he was interested in baseball?''

"What has that got to do with anything?'' he asked.

She made a face. "Ignacio caught a ride with us because he obviously wanted to sound us out, see what he thought of us. Why else would he come up to us and ask for a lift?''

Tanner looked at her like she'd lost her mind. "Because he needed a ride into town.''

She groaned. *This man is going to drive me nuts!* "He could have gotten a ride from someone else. He was checking us out,'' she insisted. "And evidently what we said about baseball got to him.''

"He just said that he played baseball when he was young. How do you parlay that into interest?''

She released an exasperated sigh. "Tanner, you need to pick up on things. Most people, men in particular, don't just come out and say 'I want to help' or even 'I want help.' You have to hear what they are saying behind their words.''

Ahead, Lucie noted the Hispanic contingent converged with the locals at Zoë's window. Riel and friends hunched up their shoulders, blocking the newcomers.

Tanner gazed at her. Finally he nodded. "I'm still learning that.''

Though distracted by the trouble brewing in front

of her—again, Tanner's humility won her admiration. *He's a good man. Maddening, but his heart is in the right place.*

"Good to hear. If you want really want to learn how to read people, you will. I think that Ignacio may prove to be a gift from God. He seems like a man who is interested in his community and isn't afraid to talk to people. Did you see how well he got on with the mechanic? They acted like old friends."

Tanner nodded. "Yes, that says a lot. Mitch wasn't too happy when the Texans started moving in."

At the order window, Riel and the Latino teen were exchanging words. Their body language made her think of wrestlers circling one another. Should she do something? But what?

Just then a sheriff's car swooped into the lot and parked near the Bomb. This arrival did not go unnoticed by the teens. The two swaggering groups of teens at the window immediately stepped apart and tried to look casual.

Following the unfolding DQ drama, Lucie tried to keep up with the topic of her conversation with Tanner. "By the way, only half our job is done. I have to get on the phone tonight and tomorrow morning and invite Mikey and Danny's friends."

"Won't we have enough to handle if kids from Shangri-La show up at the ball field?"

The deputy sheriff got out of his car and walked up to the window. The deputy gave his order and lounged against the glass wall of the DQ, eyeing the crowd of teens.

Tanner repeated his question.

Distracted, Lucie gave him an exasperated look. He really wasn't picking up on any of what was going on right in front of them. But what could she do about that? *Lord, Tanner Bond is too big a job for me!*

She tried to keep her voice calm. "We need to get the two groups together." She gestured, bringing her fingers together in a gathering motion. "If only Mikey and Danny show up, it will look like the locals didn't want to come. Another slap in the face for the Latinos."

"Ah." He nodded, getting it—finally.

"Kids are the best place to start because they have little or no prejudices. They can get the coming together off the bat." She grinned at her baseball metaphor.

At the DQ window, Zoë handed Riel and his group their order and another girl delivered the deputy's extralarge spiral cone. Riel's group headed back to their vehicle. The Hispanic kids put in their orders while the deputy lounged near the window eating his cone.

Confrontation avoided. Lucie's tension eased.

"Is it time for Zoë to be done?" Tanner consulted his watch. "We need time to make those calls."

Lucie debated calling Tanner's attention to what had just transpired in front of him—all of which he hadn't noticed. But she gave up. *I've had a long day,*

*and trying to get this man moving has made it feel
even longer.*

The deputy sheriff ambled to his vehicle. He
glanced their way and then walked over. "Evening,
Pastor."

Tanner greeted the policeman and introduced Lucie.

The deputy motioned toward the back seat. "That
the dog you hit?"

Fella barked once. Reaching over the seat back, Lucie patted his head. "Yes."

The law officer eyed her. "Does Sophie know that
Riel Wilkins is hanging around Nate's sister?"

"I don't know," Lucie said, uneasily returning his
stare.

"Well, I sure wouldn't want him hanging around
my sister."

Chapter Five

At nearly quarter past ten the next morning, Lucie was very aware of the first hot whiff of the coming summer wind and her simmering irritation with Tanner. A mix of boys and girls in two informal clusters faced each other over home plate in the city park. And these natives were restless. Oblivious, Tanner stood before them doing his let's-lecture-them-till-they-drop talk on sportsmanship.

Fuming, Lucie held herself in check. *Tanner, we need to get the practice started!*

She blew warm breath up toward her bangs. In the growing heat, they were quickly becoming moist corkscrew curls. She felt hot and sticky while her friendly neighborhood pastor, wearing khaki shorts and a short-sleeve white shirt, looked cool and collected. "I will expect you all," he was saying, "to adhere to the rules of the game...."

Lucie tried to ignore the golden down on Tanner's arms. How did a man who spent his life reading manage to have such muscular arms? Was he a closet athlete?

The kids shifted impatiently in front of her. At the diamond, the two groups, sons and daughters of the locals and the Mexican-Americans, were dressed in a rainbow of shorts and T-shirts. All the kids wore the same expression—wary yet bored at the same time. From under lowered eyelashes, they surreptitiously studied each other. Lucie prayed for unity, for friendships to begin today.

One friend had already been made. Ignacio Valdez, his silver hair glistening in the sun, lounged nearby with his arms folded. He'd shown up with a truck full of kids. Their two lone spectators, Fella and Tanner's dog Sancho, relaxed side by side in the shade of a nearby tree, ready to be entertained. Fella woofed once as though scolding the long-winded pastor. Sancho seconded it.

Impervious, Tanner continued, "I know you will avoid name-calling…"

Lucie shifted on her feet again while watching Tanner's chin move as he spoke. *Tanner, shut up—please! If you keep this up, they'll all turn tail and run home.*

"…and any other displays of poor sportsmanship—"

His deep, rich voice both irritated her and sensitized her to him—word by word, an exquisite tension. Lucie couldn't take any more.

"That's great, *padre!*," she cut him off, adopting the common Spanish parlance for his calling. "Miguel, Danny, Mikey and everybody else, I'm Señorita Lucie, your pitcher, *su lanzador*. We're going to split you all up into two teams. Everybody, line up by me."

Tanner looked shocked and then disgruntled. He propped his hands on his lean hips, his square shoulders rippling with annoyance.

The pose caught her up short. *My, you're handsome when you're angry, Tanner.* If they'd been alone, she'd have teased him with this, knowing it would get his goat. But not now. There was no time.

There was a rush of small bodies toward her. Predictably, Miguel maneuvered his way to first in line. She grinned at him. "Okay, Miguel, let's count off. You're a number one. Next kid, you're a number two." She pointed at the third kid. "You're a number one. Go on. One-two, one-two." The counting off zipped down the ragged line, splitting apart and mixing together the two bands of would-be players.

"Ones!" She motioned to Miguel's team. "You're in the field!" She glanced to Tanner who looked prepared to object. "Mr. Bond is your coach." Holding up a hand with two raised fingers, she turned to Ignacio with a lift of her eyebrows in challenge. "Twos! Señor Valdez is your coach! You're at bat. Play ball!"

Ignacio grinned at her as though reading her mind and enjoying it. He motioned the children to come to him.

She trotted toward the pitcher's mound, not giving

Bond a chance to lodge a protest. But she felt his intense and very disapproving gaze following her all the way.

After a moment of hesitation, the two teams galloped, swarming around their respective coaches. Lucie heard Miguel demand of Tanner, "*Hey!* I'm on first base, okay, Coach?" This made her glance over her shoulder.

Tanner looked stunned...and steaming. He sent her a look, as fierce as a blazing fireball. And, unexpectedly, it ignited a flickering heat in her blood. Her pulse zoomed. She stared at Tanner, trying to figure out this unexpected reaction. To regain control, she broke eye contact and located Ignacio standing by home plate.

The older man was already squatting to communicate at eye level with his team. He was talking to the kids, getting their names and shaking their hands, one by one.

On the mound, Lucie took her time warming up to pitch. While the two coaches and teams sorted themselves out, she found she couldn't keep her gaze from straying to Tanner again. Had she pushed him too far?

From the corner of her eye, she watched him. The kids clamoring around him finally brought Tanner out of his irritated trance. He started talking to his team. He was learning to roll with the punches. And she liked the way he didn't hold on to anger.

Ignacio lined up his team on the bench near home plate. He directed Danny to take the bat and he placed himself behind the boy, showing him where to grip the bat and how to swing, giving instruction on batting form to his whole team.

In the field, Tanner was obviously listening to Miguel and nodding. Then he squatted down as Ignacio had, talking to each player. *Great, Tanner!* The pastor was starting to come out of his shell.

Her heart warmed toward him. He'd obviously meant well with his opening lecture. He just needed experience with how to handle little kids.

Lucie gave the coaches a few minutes and then called out, "I'm ready to pitch. Can we play ball?"

Ignacio shouted, *"¡Sí!"*

Tanner waved. "Just a moment! We still need a catcher!"

A little blond girl with chubby legs tugged at the pant leg of his shorts. "I'm Sarah Louise Kremer," she announced. "I'm a catcher! I catch good!" With that, Tanner's team churned onto the field, leaving him at the sidelines.

"Play ball!" Lucie yelled and threw out the first pitch. Joy filled her at all the happy faces. But it was Tanner's animated expression that captured her heart.

It was nearly noon. The ice-breaker game had taken the first hour and now, under Ignacio's direction, the two teams were practicing catching and throwing. The teams faced each other and tossed balls back and forth, moving farther and farther apart. Even though they only had four balls, these provided enough action to keep the youngsters busy. Especially since none of them could catch a ball.

Looking like bobbers on a tangled fishing line, the kids stooped to pick up dropped or missed balls and then bobbed up to toss the ball again. Thanks to Ignacio's steady stream of encouraging words in English and Spanish, the kids remained eager. Soon they imitated the older man, calling to each other, "You can do it, *amigo!*" "That's okay!" "Good throw!" "*¡Bueno, amiga!*"

The glowing smiles on the kids' faces lit up the park. There had been no name-calling, no bad sportsmanship—just kids fumbling around with balls and bats and doing a lot of shouting and jumping. She chuckled. It reminded her of her summers spent volunteering with Head Start in Milwaukee. The next time she visited Shangri-La, she hoped she'd see a glimmer of this new attitude. *That's what we're here for, Lord. Bless this day with fruit.*

As an unexpected dividend, a few retired farmers in feed caps and a few of Ignacio's contemporaries had strolled over the square after their morning coffee at the café. Though keeping to two distinct factions, they lounged in the stands, watching. Some of the kids had waved and shouted, "Hi, Grandpa!" "Hey, *Abuelito!*" Lucie's heart swelled with satisfaction. The impromptu plan was already bringing the community within talking distance.

Suddenly she became aware that Tanner was staring

at her. Unable to resist reciprocating, she turned to him and felt herself blush—sizzling from toe to head.

"Okay!" she shouted to hide this disconcerting reaction. "It's nearly lunchtime! Coaches, why don't we do a practice inning until the noon bells chime?"

The kids yelled their approval and Ignacio jogged his team into the field.

Tanner grimaced. Looking as though reminded that he had a lecture ready for her, he hurried his team to the batter's bench.

You'll get your chance, Tanner. Taking a deep breath, Lucie wound up and tossed a ball to Miguel who, of course, had managed to be first at bat. Miguel's swing caught the ball with an odd "crack." The ball flew sideways.

And struck little Sarah Louise Kremer, sitting on the end of the bench. The little girl screamed and clamped her hands above one eye.

Tanner burst into the emergency room of the small rural hospital ten miles northwest of Pleasant Prairie. His heart beating a steady tattoo, he carried Sarah Louise, a small chubby armful. Lucie hurried by his side with Mikey and Danny in tow. He approached the counter. "We—" he swallowed to moisten his dry mouth "—have a little girl—"

"Is that the Kremer girl?" the receptionist asked.

"Yes." He dragged the back of his hand over the sweat on his forehead. "We called her mother at work—"

"She's on her way." A nurse stepped forward pushing a wheelchair. "We have verbal permission to examine Sarah."

Tanner tried to settle the little girl into the wheelchair.

"No!" Sarah objected, clinging to him.

He held on to her, feeling her small frame trembling. *Oh, Lord, please don't let her have a concussion.* "I'll carry her," he said, giving Sarah a gentle hug.

Lucie touched his arm and gave him an encouraging smile. "Don't worry, Sarah," she crooned, "Coach Bond won't leave you." She turned and murmured to him, "I'll take my nephews to their father's room upstairs and be right back."

In this situation so unusual for him, Lucie's presence had bolstered his confidence. He didn't want her to leave. But he understood that the boys shouldn't have to witness Sarah's examination. He nodded and Lucie walked away, shepherding the boys in front of her. It was as though she were taking the sunshine away with her.

He steadied himself, bringing his mind back to Sarah. So far, he seemed to have done what he should. They'd gotten ice from the church fridge and fashioned a rudimentary ice pack with a dish towel before heading for the hospital.

Now, at the nurse's direction, he carried Sarah to the examining table and set her down with care. The little girl held on to his arm with a tenacity that surprised him.

Her trust in him brought soothing words up from his memory, comforting words his mother had whispered to him when he'd sat in an emergency room years ago. He'd fallen from his bike speeding down a hill. He'd forgotten that episode till now. It had been a long time since he'd heard any soft, honest words from his mother. The old helpless regret filled him.

The nurse hadn't even finished taking Sarah's vitals when a middle-aged doctor walked in. "Hi, Sarah. What happened this time?"

The doctor's calm voice soothed Tanner's spiked nerves.

"I got hit by a baseball," Sarah said, "in my eye." Her lower lip quivered as she twisted the fabric of Tanner's shirt sleeve.

The doctor lifted Sarah's chin and studied her face. "Well, I'd say that sounds about right."

Tanner squeezed the girl's shoulder. "You'll be fine," he murmured.

A woman rushed into the room. "Sarah!"

Tanner watched the reunion of mother and daughter and braced himself for recriminations. After all, the children at the ball diamond had been his responsibility. *Lord, we got off to such a great start this morning. Does it end here?*

The woman turned to him. "Pastor?" She held out her hand. "Thanks for bringing Sarah straight here. I wouldn't have wanted her to have to wait at the park until my neighbor or I got there. Thanks.''

Tanner shook the woman's small, but firm hand. ''You're not upset?'' he croaked, unable to stop himself from voicing this.

She chuckled. ''Kids will be kids. It could have happened right in front of me. Sarah's my fourth. I'm a hardened veteran.'' She grinned.

''Thank you.'' Relief rushed through him.

''Thank *you!* I really appreciate that you and Sophie's cousin started the softball practice in the mornings. Our kids need something beside the pool in Dailey for fun. And it doesn't open till the afternoon.''

''We're glad to do it.'' Tanner only hoped the other parents held the same view. Or would there be fewer kids at the diamond tomorrow morning? *What's my next step, Lord?*

The doctor finished writing on the patient chart. ''Bond, you should get a medical permission form for each child. That way, we don't have to wait for a parent to get here. Mrs. Kremer was easy to get hold of and I'm their family doctor. I understand, though, that a lot of the kids are pretty much strangers around here.''

As usual, news traveled fast, so the doctor knew about the informal ball games and realized a lot of Mexican-American kids were involved.

''We, of course,'' the doctor continued, ''provide emergency medical treatment to anyone. And the kids whose parents are employed at the packing plant have medical benefits." The doctor gave him a look filled with meaning. "But since they are children, we still must get parental permission to treat them."

Tanner nodded. The doctor was emphasizing that getting permission to treat was the real issue here, not money.

"Ask the receptionist," the doctor continued. "I keep a form on file for organizations and baby-sitters to use as a guide."

"I'll do that." Feeling no longer needed, Tanner patted Sarah's arm. "See you tomorrow, Sarah?"

"If she feels good enough," Sarah's mom replied.

"She should be there," the doctor said in a hearty tone.

Waving farewell, Tanner went in search of Lucie. She'd want to know about Sarah. And he wanted to be near her again. The thought shook him, but it didn't slow him.

Lucie looked up to see Tanner enter Nate's room where Sophie and her children had gathered around Nate. His concerned expression brought her own emotions bubbling to the surface. But she kept her voice calm. "How's Sarah?"

"No concussion. Just a bump." He grinned.

She felt herself smiling, too. "Her mother came?"

"She's driving her home now." He turned to Nate, reaching out to shake his hand. "Did we catch you between therapy sessions?"

The big man, now gaunt from weeks of lying in a

hospital bed, let Tanner hold his large but limp-looking hand. Nate tried to smile. "I walked better between the bars today. My therapist tells me it won't be long before I walk out of here on crutches."

Lucie wasn't fooled. Sophie's expressive face told a different tale. Lucie had come in just in time to see Nate being wheeled back into his room. He wasn't even on crutches yet? How many weeks before he was able to come home? The occupational and physical therapy bills were mounting.

Tanner looked to Lucie. "Why don't you take Sophie and the boys to the cafeteria for lunch while I chat with Nate?"

Catching the look in his eyes, she nodded. He was telling her he'd give Sophie a break while he was there with Nate. *Thanks, Tanner.* She motioned for Sophie to precede her out the door.

With a backward glance, she said, "We need to talk, okay?" Seeing Sarah hurt this morning had reminded her of her years with Head Start. She and Tanner had omitted an important requirement for working with kids. And it was probably her fault for rushing him. *Tanner, we needed permission forms.* She hoped this accident wouldn't keep kids away tomorrow.

"After lunch," he agreed, but his attention shifted to Nate. "We had a good morning. Mikey is on my…"

Mikey and Danny took one of each of her hands and tugged her out into the hall. "We want hot dogs!"

Lucie sent one last glance over her shoulder to Tanner, grateful for his understanding that Nate needed a man to talk to. Tanner might be irritating sometimes, but he had moments when his intelligence showed itself. And the look he gave her sent a shiver through her.

She'd made the mistake of underestimating this man's effect on her. She didn't have her life planned out in minute detail in triplicate. But she had realized one truth about herself—she couldn't become involved with a clergyman. She didn't have what it took to be the perfect preacher's wife, like her mother. To her, that made Tanner Bond one dangerous man.

That afternoon, Lucie sat at Sophie's kitchen table, with Tanner across from her. Sancho and Fella lounged on the floor where the breeze came through the screen door. From outside came the distant sound of a neighbor's tractor.

Lucie tried to resist looking directly at Tanner. Just catching glimpses of him seemed to keep her on edge. Now the way his earlobe curved fascinated her.

Come on, Lucie. Get a grip. He's not a man who should interest you. He's nice enough, but you have different visions for your life, way different. And they don't include being attracted to a small-town clergyman.

The boys were outside playing with their new litter of barn kittens. Lucie sipped from her chilled glass of sweetened ice tea. It was a hot day, but to keep bills down, Sophie was trying not to turn on the air conditioner until July. This morning, Lucie had watched Sophie frowning over the checkbook as she'd paid the monthly bills.

That was one area where Lucie couldn't help her cousin. Even if she didn't spend a dime for anything but gas for the Bomb, she'd still be flat broke before July Fourth. And her muffler could fall off at any moment. But she couldn't ask Sophie for money. *Lord, help me out here. You've always provided for my every need.*

"Here's the medical permission form that I got at the clinic." Tanner slid the paper toward her. "Just to be sure it gets the message across, I'd like you to translate it into Spanish below the English and we'll pass the same form out to all the parents, today if possible."

She nodded, keeping her eyes lowered, afraid she'd forget herself and stare at him. "Sounds like a good idea. That way everyone gets the information." She cleared her throat. "And we need to add a line where the parent or guardian gives their permission for their child to participate." She grimaced. "You were right. We should have had a meeting and done all this stuff *before* we got started." She watched for his reaction to her confession.

He shrugged. "Live and learn."

He was being gracious and she knew it. "You're being kind." She paused. "Sometimes I get carried away."

He grinned at her. "Really? Not you!"

She punched his pleasantly solid biceps.

He rubbed his arm with a good-humored grimace. ''I think we should add a liability release, too.''

She propped her chin on one hand and stared at him, forgetting her desire to avoid the melting effect his warm brown eyes had on her. ''Do you think that's necessary? Did Sarah's mother threaten to sue?''

''No, but I think it would be prudent. If we mention the liability issue, it gives parents a chance to remember that we are doing this as *private* volunteers, not part of an organization that has liability insurance. So they know what to expect *if* anything serious should happen to any of the kids.''

She looked at him, her gaze lingering on the cleft in his chin. She shook herself. ''You're right.'' She hadn't given a thought to liability issues.

''I've only been here a year, but I don't think we'd have any real concerns unless we did something obviously negligent that endangered a child. Around here, people don't appreciate anyone who files lawsuits just to see what they can get. In fact, I would think that public opinion would be pretty negative toward anyone who did. Especially since we are doing this for the community—*gratis*.''

She couldn't help but be drawn to a man who cared so much about kids, about his community. ''Maybe we should buy a junior-size batting helmet.'' Then she cringed at her suggestion. She didn't have a dime to contribute to anything.

"I was thinking someone might have one an older sibling had outgrown that we could borrow."

She nodded with approval. Feeling his gaze on her, she picked up a pencil from the table. She concentrated on reading the form and writing Spanish phrases at the bottom. "Do you have a computer and printer at the church office?"

"Yes. Are you computer literate?"

She nodded, letting English phrases and their Spanish translations flow through her mind—like *hombre atractivo,* handsome man—*ojos marrón,* brown eyes.

"Word processing?" he inquired.

"Sí." She jotted a few more Spanish words on the sheet, trying to switch her mind back to the legal phrases in front of her.

"Desktop publishing?"

Where was he headed with this Twenty Questions? She looked up at him. "What's up?"

"I was wondering if you'd be interested in doing a little part-time clerical work at the church office." He looked down as if uncomfortable.

The innocent question staggered her. Her mother had been a church secretary, paid and unpaid, many times over the years of her father's pastorate. But Lucie had never contemplated doing such work herself.

Being asked to be a church secretary packed an emotional punch she hadn't expected. In her mind, it was all tied up with her resentment toward her mother for letting others take her for granted. The church members had just expected her mother to pick up the slack and that had always irked Lucie.

"You look surprised."

An understatement. Her heart pounded as though she'd just rounded home plate. Why did it upset her so?

Lucie acknowledged that this was just the type of extra work that she had felt her mother shouldn't have been asked to do when she was already so involved in her husband's ministry. But of course, Mom, being the perfect pastor's wife, hadn't seen it that way at all and she had done the typing, copying and collating without complaint. Her mother's complacence had always chagrined Lucie and now she was being asked to fill the same role.

But then another thought elbowed its way into Lucie's welter of emotions. *Dear Lord, is this Your provision?* She sighed. The answer was self-evident. She needed a flexible, very part-time job and she was being offered the perfect one. And evidently, God had had this all lined up before she'd even asked about anyone about a job.

"I didn't know," she hedged, "that St. Andrew's could afford to hire a secretary."

"Not full-time, not even part-time, just a few hours here and there. I'd like help giving the church bulletin and newsletter a new look. Your degree is in art, right?"

"Art education," she corrected him. "But I have done some graphic art and desktop publishing." She began talking to herself. *You can do this. You won't become your mother just helping out the church. And* *your bank balance is $83.15. Beggars can't be choosers.* "Well, if you think I could be of help...."

Her spirits did another unexpected free fall. Her agreeing to this only emphasized how her summer plans had gone awry. *When will I be able to start looking for a real job? I can't even send out résumés because I can't get away for interviews! The school year will be started before I'm free again!*

"When would it be good for you to come over to work?" Tanner's voice called her back.

She inhaled some of the heavy, humid air and dealt with reality. She should definitely refuse. This man drew her attention even though she knew it would never work out. With this job, she'd be with him mornings and now evenings! "How about in the evenings when Sophie's home from the hospital?" The words flowed from her lips, shocking her.

He nodded. "Great."

What have I done? Self-conscious, she looked down at the paper again and began jotting the translation. *Focus on the paperwork or you'll be lost, Lucie!* "I'll add the liability and permission notations. Can you type this or do you want me to? You'd have to watch the boys—"

"No. After you finish, I'll go over it with you so I get the spelling right. Then I'll type this, run off copies and then take them over to Ignacio. He lives with his daughter and gave me her phone number. He wanted me to call him about Sarah. I figure he'll know which kids at Shangri-La need these."

Impressed by his efficient plan, she grinned and drew a happy breath. "Hey, there's no grass growing under your feet."

He colored. "I just don't want one little accident to put the brakes on this. The kids were having a great time."

To lighten the mood and short-circuit his claim on her reactions and thoughts, she imitated Miguel's voice, the way he called to his teammates that morning. "Hey, *amigo!* I'll get this done ASAP."

Tanner grinned back at her. "Hey, *amigo* back at you!"

"Make that *amiga!* I'm a feminine-type friend," she teased.

He chuckled. *"Amiga."*

The way he looked at her sent that sizzle through her again. Morning and now evenings with Tanner. *Oh, dear.* She'd have to get over this. *Fast.*

Forcing her mind back to translating, she realized that at least, now she'd be able to afford the new muffler…sort of. Maybe Mitch would let her pay it off so much a week. She then recalled she had to go to Dailey this afternoon and pick Zoë up from the public pool there. Thinking of Zoë sent her mood downward.

Something of her frustration and worry must have shown on her face because Tanner touched her arm in a sign of sympathy.

A current zipped up her arm. Before she could stop herself, she leaned toward him, then froze. The air between them became charged. He leaned closer.

"Hi!" A cheery woman's voice jolted them. "It's me, Nella, from down the road. I brought a pie for Sophie and the kids." The woman walked in and her eyes widened as she took in Tanner's hand on Lucie's arm.

Oh, no. Lucie groaned silently. *We're in for gossip now.*

A week later, a door slammed in the night at Sophie's. At the foot of Lucie's bed upstairs, Fella woke and gave a soft bark. Lucie sat up. Midnight blackness surrounded her. Shocked out of sleep, she blinked, trying to orient herself. She heard the sound of a motor.

She threw back the covers and stumbled to the window. In the glow from the high yard light, she glimpsed a truck turning around in the yard. It looked like the truck that kid had driven when she'd been at the DQ with Tanner over a week ago! Zoë's white-blond hair glowed in the shadows as she sat in the passenger seat next to the unseen driver.

Lucie's mind lurched to an unpleasant conclusion. *Sneaking out at night? I don't think so, Zoë.*

The truck was moving slowly, quietly, out of the yard. Not wanting to wake the household, Lucie told Fella to stay. Grabbing her jeans from the back of a chair, Lucie pulled them on over her short summer pj's and headed out, snatching her purse as she went. As quietly as she could, she raced downstairs to the back door and out to her car.

Chapter Six

Lucie managed to reach the yard in time to see the pickup's red tail lights turn left onto the county highway. Her heart thudding in a sickening way, Lucie jumped into her car. She thanked God for her new muffler. Instead of roaring out to the road, the Bomb purred softly, not alerting the driver of the truck. And would anyone bet against the driver being that Riel Wilkins the sheriff had warned her about?

Driving cautiously, Lucie kept the battered pickup in sight. Finally, it turned onto a dirt road that dead-ended in a cornfield. Lucie's mouth tightened into a grim line and dread settled in her midsection like a cold brick. She'd been right to follow.

The dirt road was a narrow one, probably formed over years by a farmer moving equipment in and out of his field. Lucie parked just off the road and tried to think of how to handle this. A tremor of fear trickled through her. This was a lonely spot and darkness folded around her.

But if she read the situation right—which no doubt she had—she must take action quickly for Zoë's sake. Riel hadn't spirited the young girl away from home in the middle of the night to this deserted place to play "Go Fish" or discuss world affairs.

Pressing a hand to her throbbing temple, Lucie exhaled. *Dear Lord, protect me and Zoë. And help me out here! I'm not up to this challenge!* She chewed her lower lip, wishing she had a cell phone. But who could she call? *I'm too young to be a chaperone.* But she was the only one available.

Then she inched forward, the car rocking on the rutted track. She parked at an angle, effectively blocking Riel's exit, unless he chose to drive through the ankle-high corn in the muddy fields, which was close to each side of her car. Out of her glove compartment, she extracted a flashlight and shoved open her door. At the last minute, she pulled the hefty tire iron from under her seat. Making no effort to go unnoticed— besides, Riel must have seen her lights pull up behind him—she slammed her car door.

She snapped on the light. Aiming it at the uneven ground, she picked her way through the muddy furrows and hillocks of wild grass. Cicadas dinned in her ears. The humid night wrapped around her like a damp washcloth. When she reached the driver's side door, she illuminated the inside of the cab.

Riel let fly a string of profanity.

"Nice to see you, too." Lucie let the grim irony flow.

"What are you doing here?" Zoë snapped, her face blazing red even in the shadows.

"We both know why I'm here *and* why you're here. And remember, I wouldn't be here if you weren't."

"You should have stayed out of this," Riel threatened with menace in his voice.

With a nonchalance she was far from feeling, Lucie raised the tire iron so it could be seen and hefted it in her hand. She wouldn't be bullied. Though the sensation of what felt like giant-size butterflies, flapping around inside, unnerved her. "Zoë," she said evenly, "go get into my car."

"You can't make me!" Zoë fired up. "I'm not a baby anymore."

"She doesn't have to go with you," Riel sneered.

Lucie aimed her flashlight directly into Riel's face. The planes of his face looked harsh in the unforgiving light and shadows. His hair was artfully unkempt and his eyes burned with anger. Cursing her again, he blinked and shaded his eyes.

She tapped the door of the truck with her tire iron. "How old are you?" she asked, menace now in her voice.

Riel didn't reply.

"Zoë isn't sixteen yet," Lucie observed in a cool voice. "But you're driving so you are at *least* that—"

"Riel's eighteen!" Zoë piped up.

"Glad to hear that. Riel, there are laws." Lucie

paused to let her point sink in. "If Zoë doesn't get in my car now, I'll go home and call the sheriff—"

This time Zoë swore at her.

Though hurt, Lucie stood her ground. "Now."

Riel called Lucie several uncomplimentary names, then he swung around to Zoë. "Go on! She can't keep us apart forever." He grabbed the back of Zoë's head, yanked her face to his. He kissed Zoë roughly and then shoved her hard toward the passenger door. "Go on," he snarled.

Riel's actions spoke of such disrespect for Zoë as a person that Lucie's hand clenched around the tire iron. What was Zoë thinking? Couldn't she see what kind of jerk Riel was?

Zoë slammed out of the truck and into Lucie's car. Lucie tramped after her, not knowing what to say. She'd managed to get the girl physically away from Riel. Lucie had snatched her out of a situation that had been fraught with dangers—about which Zoë, in her innocence, didn't have a clue.

Lucie felt a little sick from the violence in Riel's manner and her own audacity in following him out to this lonely spot. *Thank You, Father, for Your protection. Please get us home safe now.*

Inside the car, Lucie waited until she was back on the county road before speaking. "Zoë," she began.

"I'm not listening to you. You made me come with you. But Riel and I are going to be together. We love each other. You can't stop us!"

The anger, rebellion and blistering venom in the

girl's tone chilled Lucie. Her tongue failed her. What could she say?

"If you and Sophie try to stop me, I'll run away! Riel and I are in love. He's the only one who loves me."

Sharper than a serpent's tooth, a thankless child! How good Sophie had been to Zoë after her parents died! How could Zoë be so blind to the danger she'd put herself in tonight? DATE RAPE flashed like bright orange neon in Lucie's mind. The urge to shake the girl surged through Lucie.

Then in her mind, Lucie heard one of her mother's favorite scriptures: "A soft word turneth away wrath." Lucie pressed down her outrage. Zoë needed most to hear the truth.

"Do you hear yourself?" Lucie asked gently. "Sophie loves you. Nate loves you. The kids and I love you. God loves you. We wouldn't do anything to make you so unhappy. We're just trying to protect you from getting in over your head. Just now, Riel didn't treat you like a person who loves you should."

Zoë hunched against the door and turned her face away, giving no answer.

This childish response sucked the wind out of Lucie. *Was I ever this young and rebellious?* She hoped not, but she did recognize her younger self in Zoë—a little.

Lord, give me words. She's so young. She doesn't understand that she's playing with fire. Another thought intruded. How would Lucie break the news of this episode to Sophie?

Near the end of the morning baseball practice, Tanner kept watch over Lucie where she stood on the pitcher's mound. Something was wrong. The woman had barely spoken all morning. And when she did speak, she only said one word at a time. And she didn't even smile. And though he hadn't realized it till today, he'd already gotten used to Lucie's smiles. The day had dimmed without them.

"Strike three!" Lucie announced in a flat tone, her usual verve missing.

Ignacio came up beside Tanner as they watched the two teams switch places on the field. "*La señorita* is not herself today."

Tanner nodded. So he wasn't the only one who felt it. Maybe Ignacio would have a clue to what might be wrong.

On the field, Miguel paused at the pitcher's mound. "You got a toothache, Señorita Lucie?" he asked loudly. "You don't look so good."

Lucie patted Miguel's shoulder. "I just didn't get enough sleep last night. You get to your base."

Miguel did as he was told, but his backward glance said plainly that he didn't buy it.

"Even the *muchacho* sees it," Ignacio commented, his arms folded in front.

Tanner shoved his hands into his pockets. "What

do you think it might be?'' he muttered from the side of his mouth.

Ignacio shrugged. ''Women. Who can understand them?''

Tanner let out a breath. *Not me.*

The older man turned from Tanner. ''You got to do something.'' He walked over to his team to get them started batting.

Me? Tanner's eyebrows lifted. What could he do? *I'm no good with women.* His failed engagement had taught him that. *I didn't even notice anything was wrong until she handed me back the ring.* He watched Lucie wind up for another pitch. Even her movements were dulled.

Lord, what do I do? Then he thought of Nate. Had they gotten bad news? He chewed the inside of his mouth, a worry habit from childhood.

The final inning of the game passed without incident and without inspiration. *Lucie, where did you go?*

Finally, the bells chimed noon. Kids surged around him, yelling, ''*¡Adiós!*'' ''Bye!'' ''See you tomorrow!''

His attention on Lucie, he still high-fived, waved and smiled at the kids.

Under the noon sun, Tanner joined Ignacio and Lucie and her nephews in gathering up the balls, bats and mitts to be stored in the church basement. *What to say? What to say?*

''Hey, Mikey and Danny, how about you come have lunch and spend the afternoon with me?'' Ignacio invited. "I'm going fishing on the river and I got poles for you. And we'll take *los perros,* the doggies, too. They'll like fishing."

Mikey and Danny jumped up and down. "Can we, Lucie? Can we?"

"Sure," Ignacio cut in, "then Tanner can take her to the café for a nice quiet lunch. She needs a break…especially if she didn't get enough sleep last night." The man gave Lucie a glance, which said "You're not fooling anyone, *señorita.*"

Tanner was caught up short. The older man had set the problem of helping Lucie squarely into his lap. No dodging permitted. Tanner felt sweat popping out on his forehead. Was it the sun? Or the idea of having lunch alone with Lucie?

"That's okay." Without her usual enthusiasm, Lucie dragged the drawstring and tightened the cloth bag that held the balls and mitts. "You guys don't have to—"

"We want to!" Tanner blurted. "You deserve a break. And we have to eat, don't we?"

Ignacio whisked the eager boys and excited dogs into his truck with a promise to deliver them all back at the farm in time for supper. As Ignacio drove away, Tanner looked across the tree-lined square at the café. At lunchtime, it would be packed with avid eavesdroppers.

Maybe they should go someplace where they could speak privately. And in this small town, that left only one option. "Why don't you come home with me? I cooked a roast beef last night and I have some left-overs for sandwiches.''

''You don't—''

''Come on. The parsonage is just behind the church.'' This woman had become a friend in the past weeks. He couldn't let a friend down—even one who drove him crazy on a regular basis. ''You'd be doing me a favor. I hate eating alone,'' he coaxed her.

''Okay.''

In his snug, red-and-white kitchen, Tanner insisted that Lucie take a seat at the table. ''And you don't have to help me. I'm capable of making a couple of sandwiches.'' Opening his fridge, he rattled off the choices. ''Wheat or white? Mayo or butter? Cheese? Lettuce?''

''White, mayo, and yes to cheese and lettuce.'' She still sounded glum.

Seeing her in his kitchen gave him an odd feeling. He ate alone so much. He moved the Bible commentary he'd been reading during his meals to the top of the fridge. He combed his mind trying to come up with a way to let her know he was interested in what was bothering her, that she could expect help. On the counter, he laid out the roast beef, Swiss cheese and opened the lettuce keeper. He breathed a silent prayer and took the plunge. ''Lucie—''

The ringing of the phone interrupted him. He crossed to answer it.

His mother's honeyed voice took him totally by surprise. He gripped the receiver. "Mother?" He almost added, "What's wrong?"

"Tanner, darling," she gushed in her usual style. "How are you?"

"Fine." He watched Lucie still slumped in gloom. Even her gold curls had lost their bounce. "How are your wedding plans going, Mother?"

"Oh, not much planning. Just a small wedding." The slightest hesitation. "In fact, something's come up. And we may push the date forward. I'll let you know what we settle on, dear."

"What came up?"

"Oh, nothing. You know how schedules change. Barry is just so busy with his agency right now. Everyone's looking to buy or sell a home."

"Okay." Even he sensed something lurking behind his mother's words. Had she decided not to remarry for the fourth time and just didn't want to say so? "What can I do for you?"

"Oh, I just called to see what you're doing."

This really got his attention. His mother never called *just* to see how he was doing. She always called to make announcements or to give advice, not to chat. *What gives?* "Oh?"

"So, what are you doing?"

Lucie sighed and the sound rippled through Tanner. The image of taking Lucie into his arms and holding her softness close shuddered through him.

"Tanner?" his mother prompted.

Dragging his mind back, he couldn't tell his mother

he was making a sandwich for a woman. It would start up the third degree. And after his mother's very vocal and very negative reaction to the breakup of his engagement, he never even mentioned dating anyone to her. And Lucie and he weren't dating. "Just getting some lunch."

"How's the church?"

"Fine. The community's growing and so is St. Andrew's." He waited for his mother to reveal her motive for calling him.

"Good." She paused as though she didn't know what to say next. "Well, I won't keep you, dear. Just wanted to hear your voice."

"I'm glad you called, Mother." He said the obligatory words, still wondering about her unrevealed motivation.

"I am, too. Goodbye, dear."

"Bye." He hung up and turned to Lucie. "That was my mother."

Lucie looked up at him. "Is she coming for a visit?"

"No." Lucie's question shocked him as much as his mother's call. "She lives in Thousand Oaks, California. We don't get together often."

"Too bad."

He turned his mind away from the puzzle of his mother's unusual phone call and back to Lucie. She sat kind of hunched over. Miguel had been right; she looked as though she were suffering with a toothache. While Tanner spread mayo on white bread, he tried to come up with conversation, a diplomatic opening, but in vain.

Finally he turned to her, set the plates with sandwiches and chips down. "Shall I say grace?" he asked as he sat down.

She nodded.

"Dear Lord, thank You for Your bounty. *Thank You for Lucie who has brought such joy and hope to Pleasant Prairie.* And for Your tender care. You never fail us. *Give me the words to help this warmhearted and giving woman.* In Christ's name, Amen."

Lucie picked up her sandwich and stared at it as though she didn't know what to do with it.

He gave up trying to come up with a smooth way of introducing his concern for her. He just put it into plain words. "Lucie, what's wrong?"

Then he watched in horror as tears sprang to her eyes. "Is it Nate?" he asked. "Did Sophie get bad news?"

She shook her head and wept harder. "Nothing's gone right this summer, and on top of everything else…"

He waited.

"I can't tell you," she finished at last. She gazed at him, trying to swallow her tears.

He reached over and touched her arm. "I'm a pastor, remember? Whatever you tell me will be kept in strictest confidence. You know that, right?"

She nodded, wiping her eyes with her paper napkin.

"I trust you, but I can't." She bit her lip. "But pray for me and Sophie's family."

He folded her small hand completely in his. He wished he were the kind of man that people confided in easily. He wished he could help this woman who had become such a part of his life in such a short time, but all he could do was promise, "I will. I will."

For the first time, Lucie was alone in the house. The boys were still with Ignacio. Sophie and Carly were at the hospital with Nate. Zoë was at DQ—or at least, Lucie sighed long and loud, she hoped Zoë was at DQ.

In the quiet, Lucie reached for the wall phone in the kitchen. As her hand touched it, it rang. She lifted the receiver.

"Hi, sis! It's me, Anna."

"Anna! How are you?"

"Fat and sassy. My morning sickness is finally over. Hey, how would you like to teach in Wisconsin? There's an opening for an art teacher at the high school near here. You could live with me and Joe until you found a place."

Lucie's heart sank. Any other time the opportunity to live near her sister and her husband would have been excellent news, wonderful news. Tears sprang to her eyes. She worked at keeping them out of her voice. "I can't get away for an interview."

There was a pause. "Nate's still that bad?" Anna asked.

"Still hospitalized."

"Should I come?" Her sister's concern radiated in her tone. "I can get away—"

"No, I'm here—"

"If you need help. If Sophie needs help—"

"You'll be the first to know." Lucie choked back more tears.

"Okay. But if you need to talk, use that calling card I bought you."

"I will. Love you, Anna."

"Love you, Lucie."

Now filled with a longing to consult the one who'd know just what to do, Lucie hung up and dialed a familiar number. There was only one person who could help, really help. She hated to add another burden, but she had no one else to turn to.

"Hello?" A soft, sweet voice answered the ring.

"Oh, Mom!" Lucie wailed. "I don't know what to do! It's Zoë."

Chapter Seven

As Lucie wound up for another pitch, she worried her lower lip. Two days had crawled by since she'd called her mother and asked for advice and help with Zoë. *I can't put this off any longer. I have to make a decision!*

Thank heavens for these daily games and Mikey, Danny and Fella. These distractions kept her sane. With a clear blue sky overhead, she pitched the ball and her mother's voice replayed in her mind. *Your father can manage without me. A few bachelor days make him appreciate me more. Of course, I'll come if you and Sophie need me.*

Lucie had known when she called that this would be her mother's response. But Lucie had always hated it when people expected Dorothy's help at the drop of a hat. *Lord, I don't want to burden my mother. She and Dad are semiretired and they deserve this time of peace. And Zoë would disturb anyone's peace of mind!*

"Strike two, Sarah." Lucie called out, and then she again ran forward and bent to pick up the ball that had fallen short on its way to her. But the catcher, Sammie Torres, was returning the ball better. His throw had almost reached her. She gave him a thumbs-up. He replied with a seven-year-old's gap-toothed grin and then squatted behind the batter.

From the stands, a mix of grandfathers shouted encouragement. Fella woofed his and Sancho beside him yipped his.

Lord, help me here. I've got to make a decision about whether Mom should come or not. And I need to know if there is anything else I can do for Zoë. Prairie heat and humidity smothered her like a moist electric blanket.

Weighed down with worry, Lucie tossed the next ball. Sarah missed. The little girl's crestfallen expression tugged at Lucie's heart. "Strike three," Lucie announced in a sympathetic tone. "That's the game."

Her downturned emotions swirled inside her.

The two teams swarmed around Lucie as she joined Tanner and Ignacio under the shady oaks by a picnic table. The warm wind puffed in her face. It was nearly July and this afternoon she had planned to take the boys to the pool in Dailey, usually a pleasant prospect. But the thought brought her no lift.

"Hey, Señorita Lucie!" Miguel hailed her. "My mom wants to see me play ball."

Lucie looked down into the boy's burnt sienna face and the lively black eyes. The little guy had become dear to her already. She ruffled his mop of straight black hair. "What?"

"My mom wants to see me play ball," he repeated in what he probably thought was a patient tone of voice, "but she can't take off work. And it's hot in the mornings. Can't we play in the evenings sometimes after *cena,* I mean supper?"

All around, the children fell silent as though awaiting her answer.

Lucie had never thought of that. *What a good idea.*

Tanner spoke up in a strong tone. "That's something Señorita Lucie, Ignacio and I will have to discuss—"

"Why?" she snapped, her mood suddenly on edge. Why was everything a big deal with Tanner? "What's wrong with having a practice in the evenings?" But her voice stilled as she encountered Tanner's we-need-to-discuss-this-first look.

She took a deep breath, trying to take the edge off her impatience. She should have expected Tanner's response. She had to say one thing for the man—he was consistent. But right now, she just didn't have the patience for this. "Kids, ask your parents if they'd like to come some evening and tell us tomorrow."

The kids nodded and shouted, "Okay!" "*¡Bueno!*"

Tanner looked irritated.

Lucie felt her own expression becoming grimly fixed. She faced him, her arms folded in front of her.

Tanner glared back at her.

Ignacio smirked at her and Tanner. He chuckled and then he laughed.

"What's so funny?" several children demanded. "What's the joke?"

Ignacio shook his head no. "See you tomorrow, boys and girls! *¡Mañana, muchachos, muchachas!*" he said, his eyes dancing.

Within minutes, only Mikey and Danny were left playing with Fella and Sancho in the shade while Lucie and Tanner confronted each other.

"So what's wrong with the parents coming to watch their kids play?" Lucie put her hands on her hips.

"It's not that there's anything wrong with it," Tanner replied. "I just think we needed to discuss it and see if it's as good an idea as it sounds."

Simmering with irritation, Lucie turned to Ignacio. "Can you see any problem with evening games? It *is* hot. And it's going to get hotter. It's cooler in the evenings."

Tanner let out a sound of disgust. "That's not the issue. Stick to the subject."

Ignacio grinned. "You two are funny." He turned with a farewell wave. "*¡Mañana!*"

Lucie stared at Tanner.

Tanner stared at Lucie.

It began to be a chore looking huffy. An image of Tanner at the pulpit on Sunday mornings intruded. He always made so much sense when he preached. Why didn't that transfer over into his everyday life? "I'll be over at seven to help you with the new bulletin,'' she declared, ending their staring contest.

"Fine.'' Tanner's voice was firm and his eyes still stormy. "I'll be here.'' The sentence came out as a challenge.

Lucie sighed. Couldn't anything be easy this summer?

That evening, in the church office, which was in the cool basement of the old brick church, Sancho snored on his rug in the corner. Tanner adjusted the ancient black fan so it would oscillate. At the same time, he tried to adjust his marked reaction to the pretty blonde perched behind his desk. He failed.

"How old is that thing?'' Lucie asked. Her voice still had an edge to it, just as it had this morning.

He looked at her, not the fan. What was the bee in her bonnet? Why didn't she let him help her? "I think it dates from about 1935. Someone replaced the cord again recently.'' He patted the metal covering over the motor and tried to release the tension he felt building inside him. "They used to make things to last.''

"Be careful,'' she said sharply. "That thing could chew off your fingers, easy. It was built before safety standards.''

Is she trying to start a fight with me? Why? Tanner studied Lucie. Her shining cap of curls brightened the room. Her subtle fragrance—a mix of suntan lotion and soap—scented the office as the fan wafted the air around. This afternoon as he'd sat down here alone at his desk writing Sunday's sermon, he'd thought about her. He hadn't wanted to. But it seemed that whenever he closed his eyes, Lucie's image came up in his mind.

"I see you're preaching on the Parable of the Good Samaritan," she commented, glancing at his sermon notes on the desk beside his computer.

"Yes." He approached her, feeling as though she were a live bomb that had to be carefully handled. He'd stewed for quite a while after this morning's dustup. Was that still bothering her?

"That's a good sermon for the town." Her tone had moderated. She picked up his notes. Her delicate hands were sprinkled with tiny gold freckles.

His throat tightened as he imagined taking her hand in his and pulling her to her feet, then… "Loving your neighbor is a good message for any town." His tone dropped, coming out low and gruff.

She nodded and recited, " 'Jesus replied: Love the Lord your God with all your heart and with all your soul and with all your mind. This is the first and greatest commandment. And the second is like it: Love your neighbor as yourself.' " She closed her eyes as if she were praying. "Do you think the ball games are doing what we wanted them to?" She looked up into his eyes.

The sight of her blue irises and upturned nose started a buzzing in his blood. He'd never been so susceptible to a woman before. And she never flirted, never even tried to get his attention. "It's a little early to tell," he managed.

"So?" she challenged him suddenly. "Have you thought about letting the kids play in the evening and invite their parents to watch? It would be an excellent way to at least get everyone together in the same place." She pouted, her pink lips puckering provocatively.

He steeled himself against leaning over and tasting them. "Sometimes that's good and sometimes that's bad," he replied noncommittally.

"How so?" She arched an eyebrow, white-gold against her tanned forehead.

"When different groups get together, there's always an equal opportunity for discord as well as harmony."

This stopped Lucie. She hadn't thought of that. She looked up into Tanner's honest eyes, which drew her.

"And I don't know if you had noticed, but over the past few years, youth sports teams have had a lot of trouble with parents who cause trouble." He frowned. "Fighting with coaches and putting pressure on their kids to win when all we want is for kids to have fun. And the tensions in this community might just find the baseball diamond as another place to stir up discord."

Tanner's words melted into her mind like sugar stirred in warm tea. Inside, she experienced the same warm thawing. Tanner was too close for her own good. "I hadn't thought about that." She lowered her head into her hand. "What can we do to prevent that?"

"I've thought about that all afternoon and I've only come up with one answer."

Caught by the intensity in his voice, Lucie glanced up into his eyes and then couldn't look away. "Yes?"

"All we can do is try it and pray. Only God can change the hearts of men. I certainly don't have that power." He stepped around the desk and touched her shoulder. "When are you going to tell me what's bothering you? You know I'd do anything to help."

Fighting her eager reaction to his touch, she dipped her chin. "It's that obvious, is it?"

He lifted her chin with his had. "Yes. Isn't there anything I can do?"

She worried her lower lip and then sighed. Gentle currents shivered from his hand through her.

She realized that her worry over Zoë was discernible to Tanner, the man who usually missed stuff right under his nose! This finally convinced her. *I'm not the one to handle Zoë. Mom has to come. I'll call her tonight.*

"I don't want to pry, but…"

"It's Zoë. She's getting into a—she's so innocent." She turned toward him. "I'm frightened for her."

Now only the corner of the desk separated them. The clock ticked in the near silence. The refrigerator in the kitchen across the hall thrummed. Outside, an eighteen-wheeler rumbled down Main Street.

Tanner took a step closer to her.

She rose to meet him.

He cupped her cheek in his palm.

From his rug, Sancho rose and yipped once, scolding them.

Stepping away, Lucie blushed.

Tanner cleared his throat. "We'd better get busy or you won't get home until midnight."

She nodded and sat down. "I'll also type up a Spanish-English announcement about evening games. How about Thursdays?"

He nodded.

She wondered if he'd been as aware of her as she had been of him.

Later, when Lucie returned home, the house was quiet. Deepest twilight hugged the horizon—gray-violet over gold. On the front porch, she found Sophie sitting alone except for Fella at her feet. Around the chairs on the wooden floor, citronella candles flickered, warding off mosquitoes. The heat of the day had at last lost much of its punch.

"Are the kids down for the night?" Lucie asked in a hushed voice while patting Fella's head in welcome.

Sophie didn't reply. She sat, staring downward.

"What's wrong, Sophie?" Lucie touched her cousin's slender shoulder.

"Nothing." Sophie's low voice revealed just how misleading her reply was.

Lucie moved closer and folded her arms around her cousin. "I want you to tell me what's bothering you— just as if I were Mom here asking you."

Sophie burst into tears. "*Everything's* wrong! I can't keep depending on neighbors taking care of the crops Nate planted. I need farm help and there isn't anyone available!''

Lucie squeezed her cousin more tightly. ''Oh, Sophie.''

''And Nate is going to be moved out of the hospital soon.'' Her cousin spoke through her tears. ''Our medical insurance has almost run out and Nate thinks we may have to sell some land to pay for his continuing care at a rehabilitation center. Oh, Lucie, I can't bear it!''

Lucie's heart sank. Selling land that Nate's family had held on to through the Depression, droughts and floods was a crushing thought. ''If he doesn't need to be in the hospital, isn't there any way we could take care of him at home instead of sending him to the rehab center?''

''I've been trying to make that work, but I've got to take care of the boys, Carly, the farm....'' Sophie bowed her head. ''If either Nate or I had someone strong enough physically to handle Nate who could come and stay and pitch in, we'd be able to manage. Nate's ready to come home. He wants to leave the hospital. If I were strong enough, able to take care of Nate at home by myself, you're right, I could just run Nate to his appointments. But it's almost impossible to find someone I could afford to live in.''

The way her cousin leaned her head wearily against Lucie broke her heart. ''And all you've got is me. I wish I could do more—''

''You take care of the boys and help with the house

and garden. You're doing enough." Sophie pulled away and wiped her eyes. "Don't you think I realize that you should be out job hunting? But you're the only one I could call on. Everyone else has their families and jobs and can't get away."

"I'm glad I'm here," Lucie said, and realized she meant it.

"I'm going to call the real estate agent and list the acres tomorrow." Sophie's voice sounded dead.

Lucie patted Sophie's arm. "Wait on that. Let me pray about it and I'll ask my parents—"

"No! I don't want to burden your parents. They've done enough for me. When I was a kid, I would have been so lonely if they hadn't let me come and stay with you and your sisters every summer." Sophie gripped her hand.

Everything Sophie revealed strengthened Lucie's resolve not to tell Sophie about Zoë's escapade with Riel the other night. "Okay, I won't call them about the money, but please give me a day or two to pray about this. And Mom *is* coming for a visit. I just talked to her recently." She was very relieved that she'd called her mother from the pay phone before she'd left town tonight.

Sophie sighed, giving a sound of total defeat. "Okay, I'll wait a day or two. But it won't do any good. The insurance is running out and there's no money in the bank. All we've got is the land."

Lucie squeezed Sophie once more and then sat down in the wicker chair beside her. *Dear Lord, please bring Mom soon. And what about the money for Nate's care? I know You can provide. Please help Sophie find a different way to get the money. But make it plain, Lord, because my mind feels jumbled right now!*

The next day, Tanner and Ignacio had the kids running laps around the diamond to finish up their morning practice. They panted, huffed and called to each other.

''After all this running, they'll all be quiet and well behaved for their *madres* all afternoon,'' Ignacio observed with a wry twist. He stood with Tanner and Lucie under the shade of a wide, green-leafed oak.

Tanner nodded, but beside him Lucie was again sunk in her uncharacteristic gloom. Had something else occurred since last night?

Ignacio cocked an eyebrow at him and gave a trace of a nod toward Lucie.

So Ignacio had noticed, too. Tanner picked up the unspoken question and returned a bare shake of his head. This couldn't go on. This morning, even the kids had been eyeing her.

The kids rounded the final lap and rushed their coaches. Tanner followed Ignacio's lead and spoke to each of his players; all the while his mind mulled over Lucie's low spirits.

''Hey, Coach!'' Miguel called out. ''My mother still wants to see me play! Can't we come here after supper tonight and play?''

The other children joined in, clamoring their agreement with Miguel's idea.

"Here you are, *muchachos, muchachas.*" Ignacio lifted the folder of brightly colored announcements. "Take these home. Starting July sixth, parents can come every Thursday night."

"Yah!" Miguel shouted and pumped one arm skyward. *"¡Gracias!"* Then he mounted his bike and waved goodbye. All the other children climbed onto bikes or ran to waiting cars. Even Mikey and Danny drove off to spend the afternoon with friends.

Soon, only Tanner and Ignacio remained. They turned to Lucie. Ignacio nudged Tanner's arm and then went about gathering up the canvas bags of balls and bats.

Tanner forced himself to take a step closer to her. "Lucie, what's up? I thought you were feeling better last night after we talked."

She glanced up and paused, looking as though coming to a decision.

Tanner searched his mind. "It's not right to keep troubles to yourself, not if a…neighbor offers a hand." He didn't like the way his words came out, as though he didn't know what to say.

Lucie chewed her lip. "I don't know if you can help. It's Sophie…and Nate."

"Lucie, trust me."

The tone of Tanner's rich voice touched Lucie. She took a step closer to him. She might as well tell him.

Everyone would know when the For Sale sign went up.

"Nate's insurance money has nearly maxed out. Sophie is going to sell some of their land to pay for his continued care at the rehab center. If I can't come up with an idea, she's going to list the property tomorrow."

"Ay caramba," Ignacio murmured beside her. "How come the insurance money ran out so quick?"

"Farmers are self-employed," Lucie explained, "so it was an individual policy and he's young. They weren't carrying enough coverage. And the drunk driver who caused the accident didn't have insurance."

"And," Tanner added, "it was a really bad accident. Nate was on a tractor when he was hit. For almost two weeks, we didn't think Nate was going to make it."

"Sophie says," Lucie continued, "she could bring him home now, but she isn't strong enough to care for him at home by herself. He's still light-headed and unsteady on his feet. If he started to fall... She's too small to be able to help him up and down the stairs to the bathroom or in and out of the shower...."

"Can he come home?" Tanner asked. "I mean, doesn't he still need physical and occupational therapy?"

"Sophie says she could always take him to the hospital or the long-term care facility for that—"

"So *la señora* only needs help at home?" Ignacio clarified.

"Well, she also needs someone to work the fields," Lucie added.

"I think Nate should come home." Tanner nibbled the inside of his mouth. "Nate's really depressed being inside all the time. I think he'd do better at home."

"I agree," Lucie said, "but I'm not strong enough to move him around. He's six foot five in his stocking feet and still weighs around two-thirty." She shrugged with her palms out.

"I could manage him," Tanner said.

Silence.

"I could manage him," Tanner repeated. "Why couldn't I come and stay until Nate can handle himself better?"

Lucie stared at him.

"I could come, too," Ignacio said. "It would be an honor to help the father of two fine boys as Mikey and Danny."

Lucie gazed at both of them. Her mind raced. Would Sophie agree? Would it be enough? "You're wonderful!" She leaped up and hugged Ignacio, then Tanner. The feel of his broad shoulders against her hit her with undiluted force. *Why do you keep coming to my rescue? I'm liking you too much, Tanner. And that's got to stop!*

Sophie drove the minivan close to the back door of their farmhouse. Tanner, Ignacio and Lucie waited at the bottom of the steps. Tanner hurried forward to open the door of the vehicle. "Great to see you out of that hospital! Here, I want you to meet Ignacio Valdez, a good friend and neighbor."

As Nate shook Ignacio's hand, the older man said, "Let's get you inside, *amigo*."

"That won't be too easy," Nate grumbled.

"No problem." Tanner pulled the crutches from behind Nate's seat. "Let's see you handle these."

"I'm still pretty clumsy. My equilibrium is the problem. My muscle strength is coming back, but I still get dizzy."

"Tanner will walk behind you," Ignacio suggested, "and I'll walk in front. If you start to lean too far either way, we'll get you back on track, *sí?*"

Nate grinned suddenly. "*Sí.* All I want is to be back in my own place."

"I understand." Ignacio held his hands out in front as the big man struggled to get upright from the car seat. "I feel the same way each night when I get myself settled into my recliner. Ah, the comfort!"

Obviously unsteady, but determined, Nate slowly heaved himself onto the crutches and covered the short distance to the back steps. He eyed them for only a moment. "Can you hold one crutch?"

Ignacio took it.

"I'm still right behind you," Tanner reassured him.

"Okay." Nate hoisted himself up one step at a time, using the railing and one crutch.

Lucie held her breath as he made it up one, two, three and finally the last step.

"Made it." Nate breathed long with relief.

The entourage followed the man who towered over all of them into the living room where he lowered himself into his favorite armchair. He sighed with pleasure. "Wow."

Mikey and Danny swarmed up onto his lap like eager puppies. "You're home! Daddy's home!"

Lucie couldn't look at Nate's face. The raw joy and pain mingled in his expression made the glib, cheery words she was about to speak catch in her throat. She left the room and hurried outside. On the back porch, she became aware that Tanner had followed her.

"I wanted to give them a moment," he explained, stepping beside her.

"Thank you," Lucie murmured, feeling the tears begin to start in her eyes. "Thank you." Before she could stop herself, she kissed Tanner dead center on his mouth!

Chapter Eight

The luscious scent of candy cotton hovered over the Fourth of July carnival in Dailey. Lucie bumped shoulders with what looked like half the county's population crowding the fairway on the county fairground. She and Tanner walked side by side with Mikey and Danny who bounced around and between them like Mexican jumping beans.

Her plan for the day was to have fun. After several tense days of worry, help had come in the form of Tanner and Ignacio. In only two days with Nate home, Sophie looked calmer. And the FOR SALE sign had been forestalled.

Lucie tried to keep her eyes from straying toward Tanner but as the day heated up so did her attraction to…to this preacher. *This can't be happening. I can't really be interested in a minister. And I can't believe I kissed him. But it's just due to circumstances. We're*

*together for ball practice, church office duties and
now he's staying in the spare bedroom next to Nate
and Sophie's room. It's like a conspiracy—we're together 24/7. I can't get away from him! Help!*

Wearing a big smile, Sophie pushed Carly in her
stroller. The smile was due to Nate finally being per-
suaded to attend the fair. Tanner had, in the end, been
the one to get Nate to agree to come. Nate hadn't
wanted to see the fair from the rented wheelchair or
maybe it was he didn't want to be seen?

Lucie heard again Tanner's words to Nate this
morning, gentle words that overcame Nate's reluctance to be seen by his friends in a wheelchair—
"Nate, your family needs to have you with them.
You're doing this for them." And Tanner's urging had
won the day. The man definitely had his moments.
*That's why he's so dangerous to me. I've got to get
out of this town as soon as I can!*

An older couple, another in a steady succession of
acquaintances and well-wishers, stopped to shake
Nate's hand. "Great to see you here, Nate." The husband, Mort Hazelton, slapped Nate's shoulder. "We
heard that the preacher was helping out so you could
come home."

"We've been praying for you, but I'll be bringing
a meal over this week, too," Mort's wife joined in.
"Now don't say no."

"We only live a couple miles west from Nate and
Sophie's, Preacher," the husband said. "If you need
any help, call me and I'll come right over. I rented out

my fields this year. Had heart surgery in January, but I can still help out with Nate if you need a break.''

''Thank you,'' Tanner replied, ''but the other softball coach, Ignacio Valdez, is taking turns with me staying over at Nate's.''

''Is he one of those new people out at Shangri-La?'' the wife asked.

Lucie sensed the standoffishness in the question and opened her mouth to let the woman know what she thought of that attitude.

''Yes—'' Tanner cut her off ''—he's great with the kids.''

The urge to kiss Tanner a second time rocketed through Lucie. *This has got to stop! Tanner and I are like oil and water.*

''Well, I told the guys at the café,'' the retired farmer said, ''that the people at the trailer court are probably just like us—some keepers, some losers.''

Tanner nodded.

Lucie watched for the wife's reaction to this, but the woman turned her head to coo at Carly.

''I can't thank Ignacio enough.'' Nate spoke up. ''He's taken our boys fishing at the river more than once. He's really good with them.''

The crowd surged around Sophie's family and the older couple waved and moved off on the crest of people wending their way toward the food tents.

''I wanna ride that.'' Danny pointed toward the Ferris wheel towering above the fairway.

''Oh, I don't think—'' Sophie started.

"Why not?" Nate asked, out of the blue. "I'd like to ride the Ferris wheel myself."

"But Nate—" Sophie started.

"Why not?" Lucie agreed. "Nate is capable of sitting in the seat on the Ferris wheel. Let's get in line."

Tanner gave her a look, one of his please-think-before-you-speak ones.

In return, Lucie gave him one of her let's-get-this-moving expressions.

He shook his head and mouthed, "Mind your own business."

Lucie stuck the tip of her tongue out at him.

Silence.

Sophie touched Nate's arm. They exchanged glances, then her worried expression lifted. "I'm in the mood for it myself. And it would be the boys' first time."

Lucie sent Tanner an I-told-you-so look.

He ignored it.

They all moved forward, heading toward the line for the ride.

Out of the corner of her eye, Lucie glimpsed a group of teens from Shangri-La. Some of them she recognized as older brothers and sisters of the kids in softball. As they passed close by, she waved to them and smiled. Though the teens had shyly greeted her when they had picked up younger siblings, now they ignored her. *I'm probably not "cool" enough to notice in public.*

Then she spotted Riel Wilkins and his cronies peacocking their way down the fairway, too. Both groups eyed one another across the milling crowd. The looks were not friendly. Zoë had lucked out and had the holiday off from DQ. She somehow managed to walk draped against Riel.

Sophie must have noticed Zoë, too. "Zoë!" she called "Zoë!"

The girl ignored Sophie.

With a sinking sensation, Lucie could only be glad that help was on the way.

Tanner led them to the ticket line for the Ferris wheel. The jangling carnival music, the thrum of the Ferris wheel engine and the creaking of its metal parts filled Lucie's ears. Trying to shake Tanner's sway over her emotions, she closed her eyes and breathed in the mingled aromas of funnel cakes and popcorn. It didn't work. Her eyes opened and immediately sought Tanner. She caught the full force of his handsome profile.

With her artist's eye, she began to sketch his straight nose, firm chin and the clean planes of his cheekbones. He had the face of a Renaissance noble. She tore the page off her mental sketch pad and focused on the scene before her.

The Ferris wheel had started letting couples off and on, one by one. The seats filled up slowly, each one moving up and waiting for the next couple to get situated. Lucie started a conversation with Sophie about their garden, ignoring Tanner or trying to.

Finally Tanner bought tickets for everyone and

helped Nate into the seat. Beside him, Sophie took the boys onto their laps for the ride.

"Would you and Tanner take Carly up with you?" Sophie motioned to Lucie.

"I'll just stay down here and watch her sleep in the stroller," Lucie hedged, not wanting to be alone with Tanner for the duration of the ride.

"No!" Mrs. Hazelton, who'd appeared behind them, objected. "I'll watch that baby. You and your young man go up and have fun." The woman patted the baby sleeping in the stroller and nudged Lucie into the Ferris wheel seat.

My young man! Lucie squeezed her eyes shut, cringing at the implication of this comment.

She felt the seat sway as Tanner parked his solid form beside her. There was something disturbing about having him so near. He made her feel so feminine, so delicate—sensations that were completely different from the way she usually felt about herself.

"All full!" the carney shouted.

Lucie felt the seat vibrate as it rose in the air. The music, an old show tune, tinkled up around them. She watched the ground recede. In the distance, she saw Riel swaggering by with his arm still around Zoë.

As the Ferris wheel ascended, Tanner looked to Lucie. "This is my first ride on a Ferris wheel."

Her eyebrows touched her hairline. "Your first?"

"My mom didn't like carnivals. Sometimes, I'd see the Ferris wheels from the road as we drove by." He nodded toward the view. "It's breathtaking, isn't it?"

Lucie stared into the endless blue, away from Tanner, trying to ignore the brush of his arm against hers.

"You never speak about your mother." *Why did I say that? It's none of my business.*

"Nothing to say." He shrugged.

But the way he shrugged belied his words.

Don't ask. He's not your concern. Neither is his mother. "My mother's coming next week." She sat back, making the seat rock. Her mother had wanted to come immediately but her father had insisted that the car needed work before he would let her drive the distance alone. And their mechanic was on vacation until Monday.

He raised his eyebrows this time. "With your mother, we're going to have a full house."

She nodded, unwillingly studying his muscular thighs, shown off by his neatly pressed navy blue shorts. "It's good Nate's family believed in building a large farmhouse. But she'll share my room." *He even presses his shorts! I take mine out of the drier damp, shake them and that's it.*

He glanced down at her. "You never speak about your mother." He echoed her words. "Sophie does, though. I take it your mother—"

"Dorothy. My mom's name is Dorothy." *Now, Mom presses Dad's shorts.* She'd approve of Tanner's neat appearance. She'd always despaired of Lucie's casual way with laundry.

"I take it Dorothy was a second mother to Sophie?"

"Yeah." Lucie began swinging her feet. Their seat

swayed back and forth with her rhythm. Unraveling the attraction Lucie felt for Tanner would be easier with her mom here. Her mom would be a visible reminder that Lucie didn't have what it took to even date a minister, much less fall in love with one. *I'm not spending my life ironing!* "Everybody loves my mom."

"You make it sound like that's bad."

She sighed at herself. "It's not bad. My mom is a great person. But people take advantage of her. She's so sweet, so kind, so…the perfect pastor's wife." It sounded like a lame response to her own ears.

"Ahhh," he commented.

"What does that mean?" She made a face at him.

"I've heard that PKs, preacher's kids," he said, looking away, "don't like having to be perfect."

"Well, I was never in danger of being that," Lucie said with a sardonic twist of her lips.

But I also never flirted with disaster like Zoë is. Below her, she glimpsed Riel and Zoë with his group of hangers-on heading straight for the large group of Mexican-American teens she'd seen before. Their body language shouted confrontation. *No, don't spoil the day!*

Just as panic ignited inside her, she saw a county deputy sheriff walking near the two groups who were just about to collide. The two sets of teens visibly recognized the presence of the law and veered off course. *Whew!*

But the carnival setting was the perfect venue for

teenaged hormones to spark a fight. *Lord, please don't let angry young men disturb this holiday. And please keep Zoë safe when fists are flying.... Please bring Mom here safe and soon.*

"Did your mother have unrealistic expectations for you?" Tanner asked.

With Zoë's rebellion right in front of her, Lucie considered this. Images from the past came up in her mind—toe-to-toe battles she'd had with her mother over things such as wearing a bright pink miniskirt to church on Easter Sunday, getting her ears double-pierced, dating a boy who had spiked hair. Why had she thought such minor things mattered so much?

But of course, the *things* hadn't been the issues; her independence from her mild-mannered pastor's-wife mother had been. But how could she tell Tanner that? "Not really," Lucie admitted. "I just wanted to be me."

He looked puzzled and then his face cleared. "Ah."

"What do you mean, 'Ah'?" His know-it-all tone grated on her. "I didn't like how you said that."

"Well, you know," he temporized with a wave of his hand, "you have a...very...flamboyant...streak... sometimes." Then he had the nerve to look at her as if she might pop a cork—if she had a cork.

"And you, Tanner Bond—" she punched his biceps "—have a...very...stick-in-the-mud...streak...some-times."

"You're entitled to your opinion I suppose."

Then hoping to disconcert him, she grinned and pumped her feet as though she were on a park swing. Their seat rocked back and forth as it neared the ground again. "Oh, really?"

Tanner gave her a long look. "Yes."

As their seat began another ascent, he imitated Lucie and pumped his legs. They swung forward and then rocked backward. His legs proved longer and more powerful that hers.

"Ohhhhh!" Lucie wailed, her stomach churning.

Tanner repeated the motion.

Lucie shrilled, "Tanner! I could lose my lunch!" She grabbed his arm.

"I'm not a stick-in-the-mud!" he taunted her. "Say it!"

"You are!"

He pumped again. Their seat swung to its maximum, back and forth.

"Okay! Okay!" Lucie shrieked. "You're not a stick-in-the-mud! Uncle! Uncle!"

Then she heard laughter from above her. Sophie and Nate were laughing at them! The sound of Nate laughing lifted Lucie's mood and she laughed at herself.

Shifting on tired feet, Lucie waited for the fireworks to begin. It had been a long, hot Fourth of July and Tanner had left to take Nate, Sophie and Carly home and feed the dogs. Lucie imagined crawling into bed—what a welcome thought!

Mikey and Danny leaned against her, also fatigued

but not willing to give in. ''How much longer?''
Mikey asked.

Lucie glanced at the growing darkness. ''Not long
now.'' Tanner had said he'd come back to help her
get the boys home. She'd told him not to bother, but
now she wished she hadn't. She missed him. If he
were beside her now, she'd have been tempted to rest
her head on his chest. Just thinking the thought
warmed her to her toes.

Then it's good you told him not to come back. Re-
ally, Lucie, you're not being logical. You know you
have to get rid of these idiotic feelings—

Suddenly she noticed that Sam Torres, the man who
had slammed a door in her face that night she and
Tanner had gone to the mobile home court with Fella,
was heading straight for her. He was a formidable-
looking man and had the same scowl on his face that
he'd had at their first meeting. What could he want?

He came to a halt in front of her. ''Señorita Lucie?''

''*Sí.*'' She felt a shiver of apprehension streak
through her. Would he ask for his dog back? She
hoped not. She'd come to love Fella.

''I hear your cousin needs help on her farm?''

Lucie nodded.

''I worked on farms in Texas, not corn and soy-
beans, but I know how to spread herbicide and run the
equipment. I could come in the evenings or the weekends.''

Lucie could hardly take in what the man was saying.

His offer didn't fit her preconceptions of the man. "We can't pay much."

"I just want to work outside—not sit in the trailer when I'm off work," he said gruffly. "I like working the land."

Lucie swallowed. "Why don't you come over tomorrow after work and talk to Nate? He's the one you want to talk to."

"*Bueno*. I will. *Gracias, señorita*." He looked like he wanted to say more, but right then another familiar voice summoned her.

"Hey! Señorita Lucie! This is my mom!"

Lucie glanced over and saw Miguel dragging a plump, dark-haired woman, dressed in jeans and a floral print peasant blouse, toward her.

Sam Torres nodded and turned away.

After saying *adiós* to Sam Torres, Lucie smiled and offered her hand to Miguel's mother. "*¡Hola!*"

"I'm Maria." The woman shook her hand. "I'm happy to meet you. Miguel talks about you all the time."

Lucie ruffled Miguel's dark hair. "You have a wonderful son. He's our most enthusiastic player."

Maria chuckled. "I'll bet. I want to thank you for taking an interest in Miguel. It's hard for him to be alone all day with just his older brother watching him. I was hoping Juan would be able to find a job this summer, but..." Maria shrugged. "But I needed someone to watch Miguel anyway."

Lucie didn't want to say anything, but if an older

brother was watching Miguel this summer, it was news to her. But she just gave Maria a tight smile.

"Here," Maria explained, "Juan plays video games all day and runs around all night. At home in Texas, he always helped his grandfather at his small engine-repair shop in the summers. But the recruiter from the packing plant told me about the great schools here. I wanted that for my boys." The woman wiped a smudge off Miguel's chin with her fingertips.

Lucie wondered why people always told her personal information like this. Lucie's father had told her that people confided in her because she looked like someone they could trust. Whatever the reason, it was obvious that Maria was worried about her older son. Maybe she didn't have anyone else to talk to about this. Or maybe she thought Lucie could help her with advice. *I'm not up to this task, Lord.*

"Miguel says that the *padre* is really nice—once you get to know him?" Maria posed the statement as a question. The woman studied her, no doubt waiting for Lucie's response.

Maybe Maria thought Tanner could help with Juan, too. Lucie nodded in reply—though she didn't know what Tanner would do with Juan. He hadn't known what to do with Miguel. Lucie suddenly remembered that Tanner had said that the church mower needed fixing. "Did you say Juan was mechanical?"

"Why, *sí*, yes, he is."

Bingo! Thank you, Lord. "Why don't you have him

drop over after Friday's softball practice and he can take a look at the church's lawn mower."

Maria beamed at her. *"¡Estupendo!"* The woman scanned over the crowd. "There he is. There's my Juan."

Lucie followed the woman's motion and saw a young teenaged male in scuffed cowboy boots and faded jeans slouching near the front of the group of similar-looking teens, the same group that had been on a collision course with Riel's crowd earlier.

Again, this wasn't something she was going to tell Maria. It could sound like a criticism of Juan. She turned her gaze back to the woman. "So how about you, Maria? Have you adjusted to life in Pleasant Prairie?"

Maria shrugged. "I go to work. I come home and clean house and cook. There's not much to do around here."

"Sometimes," Miguel piped up, "we drive to Des Moines on Saturday to see a movie or go to the mall."

"Sí, but there isn't much of a social life here," Maria finished.

Lucie nodded. Pleasant Prairie's social life centered around family and church. If a person didn't have a large family or belong to a church, one didn't have much opportunity to socialize. *Tanner and I need to talk about this.* "Well, we hope you'll come and see Miguel play ball two nights from now."

"I'm looking forward to it." Maria put her arm

around Miguel's shoulder and gave him an affectionate squeeze.

Overhead, the first skyrocket burst into streaks of magenta and gold. Oooooh's and Aaaaah's began as everyone looked skyward.

"Wow!" Miguel breathed. "I'd like to shoot off one of those."

"Me, too!" Danny agreed in an awestruck voice.

"Me, too!" Mikey agreed.

The explosions of bright colors—crimson, gleaming white, royal blue and the all the shades of the rainbow—kept the crowd enthralled for nearly a half hour. Then the grand finale swooped above them, deafening, dazzling and very welcome. It was time to go home and get the boys to bed. Lucie was beat. She took the boys by the hand and scanned the crowd for Tanner's face. Maybe he'd taken her at her word and had decided not to come back.

Sudden shouts. Many voices. "Catch him!" "He's got my purse!" "Don't let him get away!"

A scream.

Lucie pulled the boys close to her sides and tried to get out of the way. Juan was running straight at her.

Maria shouted, "Juan, stop!"

Someone put out a foot. The teen went down. The crowd surged around him.

Then Tanner was there, pushing people back, helping Juan to his feet. "Step back," Tanner shouted. "Everyone stay calm."

Tanner helped Juan to his feet.

Lucie's heart pounded. *Thank heavens, Tanner came!*

"Where's the purse?" someone demanded, and others echoed him.

"What purse?" Juan protested. "I don't have anyone's lousy purse." To show proof of this, the youth held his arms wide and rotated with a cocky stance.

A deputy pushed his way through the crowd. "Sheriff's department! Let me through!"

People fell back. Lucie didn't. She stayed close to Tanner and motioned Maria and Miguel to come near her. She didn't say anything, though. From Tanner's expression, Lucie was certain he would defend Juan.

A woman, whom Lucie didn't know, wearing a red-white-and-blue shirt and jeans, followed the deputy. They both reached Juan. Tanner drew closer to the teen.

Lucie was so proud of Tanner. He stood there, ready to make sure Juan wouldn't be railroaded.

"Is this the young man who snatched your purse?" the deputy asked.

The woman in red-white-and-blue stared into Juan's face.

Lucie held her breath and put a hand on Maria's shoulder.

"No, no, I don't think so," the woman replied.

"But he was running!" people around chorused. "He must have ditched it!"

"Why were you running, son?" the deputy asked.

"I went to the john, man," Juan said, pointing back

in the direction from where he came. "And when I came out, that Riel kid was waiting for me and he wasn't alone. I wasn't going to let him and his friends beat me up, so I started running, to get to my friends. He must have been watching me…." Juan flushed under the garish carnival lights. "I don't have nobody's purse!"

"I found a purse!" A young man came forward and offered it. "Is this yours? I found it on the ground back there."

The woman took the denim purse and opened it. "It's mine, but my wallet's gone." She grimaced. "Lucky for me, I didn't carry any credit cards today. And I only had a few dollars left, but now I've got to get a new driver's license. Darn."

"So this teenager didn't snatch it?" the deputy asked, motioning toward Juan.

Lucie waited for her answer. Was this over or not?

She shook her head. "No. I thought he did because he was running. I came out of the ladies' room and I skirted around this group of young guys. I was jostled from behind and felt my purse yanked off my shoulder. Then I saw this boy running. So I thought it must have been him who grabbed my purse."

The deputy let out a sound that was a cross between a sigh and a huff. "Okay, then. Everyone break it up. Go on home. The excitement's over."

Lucie felt relief for Maria and her sons flowing inside her.

But Maria took a few steps forward and confronted

the woman. "You shouldn't have accused my son! You just did it because we're Mexican-American! That Riel Wilkins is worse than any of our kids and he's right from here!"

Strained, embarrassed silence greeted this. Even a newcomer like Lucie couldn't argue with the truth of Maria's accusation.

Standing on the pitcher's mound, Lucie took a deep breath. Thursday night had arrived two evenings after the Fourth of July carnival and all the excitement over the purse snatching. She and Tanner had discussed what, if any, effect that incident might have on the game tonight. Lucie couldn't know, of course, if it had any effect or not.

But the city square was as crowded tonight as it was on Sunday mornings when both churches filled up with worshipers, or Friday nights when everyone came out to shop and eat at the café. Tonight, she certainly hadn't expected to see the stands packed with parents from Pleasant Prairie and from Shangri-La. They were filled—yet separated into two groups. Was the turnout a show of support for the kids or an act of defiance?

Along with the rest of the kids, Mikey and Danny stood proudly with their teams. The boys had ridden over with her, but Nate and Sophie had promised to follow soon.

Ignacio waved to her and then so did Tanner.

With a prayer for God's blessing on tonight's experiment, she wound up and released the first ball. The young players started the game with marked enthusiasm, which progressed to excitement. The first inning ended and the second started. Parents on one side or the other clapped as their kids made it onto base. When Miguel made it to home plate, the one half of the stands erupted into an impromptu wave.

Lucie kept an eye out for Nate's truck. Where was Sophie?

Chapter Nine

Lucie kept tabs on the two factions in the stands—the homegrown Pleasant Prairie families and the Shangri-La parents. Under the violet-tinged sky, she tried to gauge what were their attitudes to each other and their collective purposes for coming. Had this been a good idea or would the evening turn ugly?

Lucie's confidence that the evening games would be a good idea had been shaken by the unpleasant exchange after Juan had been accused of purse snatching. Would Tanner's concern be proven true?

Oh, Lord, don't let it happen! Let harmony begin tonight. Let each of the people here from the youngest to the eldest begin to feel and behave like the neighbors they are—like the good neighbors You want them to be!

She looked over and found Tanner's eyes upon her. His attention made her blush. She merely nodded, reeling in the urge to walk over to him. *He's only con-cerned about the situation, just like me!* He waved.

She waved and saw that Sam Torres was in the stands. Last night, he'd come to talk to Nate about working on the farm for the rest of the season. Nate had taken him on trial and the man was to come on Saturday and tend the fields and do some light main-tenance on the farm equipment. Lucie hoped this would work out. Maybe Sam Torres just didn't like working in the packing plant. She didn't blame him. Would doing work he liked help? She still had hopes that Fella and little Sammie would be reunited, though the little dog was welcome to stay.

Then out of the corner of her eye, she saw Nate's minivan pulling up into the handicapped parking spot nearest the field. She motioned toward the vehicle and Tanner caught her message. He immediately jogged over to it and got the wheelchair out of the rear. Lucie was so busy trying to pitch and trying to watch Nate get into his chair that she was taken by surprise by a familiar voice hailing her. "Lucie! Lucie!"

It was her mother.

Lucie dropped the ball and ran to hug her. "Mom!" Recognizing her mother's familiar perfume and feel-ing her soft cheek against her own touched Lucie. "I'm so glad you're here."

"Lucie, dear," Mom said, squeezing Lucie closer.

"You got here early!" Lucie exclaimed, joy plus relief overflowing into tears. Now she could rest easy about Zoë. Mom would know what to do.

"Our mechanic got back early from vacation and was able to get the car checked out for me this morning." Dorothy gave her another squeeze. "So here I am. We left Sophie and the baby at home to enjoy some peace and quiet. We even unplugged the phone and told her to rest."

Lucie blinked back the tears, hoping they'd go unnoticed.

Miguel appeared at Lucie's elbow. "Hey! Who's that? And what about the game?"

Wiping away her tears with her fingers, Lucie looked down and smiled. "Sorry. This is my mother, Miguel. She's come for a visit. I had to greet her!"

Miguel tilted his head a little to one side and studied Dorothy. "You don't look like Lucie's *madre.*"

Dorothy laughed. "That's because I think she looks like her *padre.*"

"Oh," Miguel said. "Can we get the game going again, Señorita Lucie?"

"Sure." Lucie walked backward a few steps, then turned and jogged to the pitcher's mound.

"I'll go sit and watch." Dorothy began to walk toward the stands. "Hit a home run for me, Miguel!"

Back on the pitcher's mound, Lucie checked to see that Tanner had retaken his place near the bench also. Nate sat in his chair in front of the stands.

Then another surprise—Lucie noticed that her mother had crossed the invisible line and had taken a seat at the edge of the Shangri-La section. Had Nate said something to Mom on their way? Or had her mother merely sized up the situation herself? Would this ease the situation or not?

As Lucie pitched one ball after the other, she kept track of her mother's progress. One by one, Dorothy greeted the Mexican-Americans around her. Lucie noted how their initial reluctance gave way under her mother's gentle conversation. And then Dorothy turned and greeted the Pleasant Prairie folks on her other side.

By the time Lucie pitched the first ball in the seventh inning, her mother was busy introducing the people on either side of her. Across the invisible line, hands were being shaken. Hesitant, but friendly nods were being exchanged. Lucie's heart sang. *Thanks, Mom! Thank you, Lord!* A grin Lucie couldn't squelch lifted her face for the rest of the game.

When the final out was called, the parents streamed down from the bleachers. But instead of gathering up their children and leaving, they milled around the field. Most came up and greeted Lucie as well as Ignacio and Tanner, thanking them for volunteering for their children this summer. Though the two groups didn't mix, the uneasiness that had permeated the crowd at the beginning of the game had softened.

Finally, Lucie had a chance to introduce Ignacio and Tanner to Dorothy. Lucie tried to be as nonchalant as possible so her mother would have absolutely no reason to assume that Tanner was more than a friend.

Dorothy offered Tanner her hand. "I'm so glad you were able to help Nate and Sophie out." Dorothy rested her hand on Nate's shoulder. "He's like a son-in-law to us."

"No problem." Tanner looked embarrassed.

"Tonight is my night with you, *mi amigo*." Ignacio clapped Nate's other shoulder.

"Glad to have you," Nate replied. "But as tired as I am, I doubt you'll hear a peep from me until morning."

"You'll get your strength back before you know it," the older man said. "In the hospital, they don't let you sleep, but they also don't let you do much. Lying around with no real shut-eye can weaken a man. But you're *joven,* young. You'll bounce back."

Lucie prayed Ignacio's word would prove true.

Nate only gave a half smile in reply. But already he looked stronger than the day he'd first come home.

"We'd better get home then," Dorothy said. "I drove all the way from Wisconsin today and I'll admit it, I'm tired, too."

"I'll follow you," Ignacio said, and proceeded to wheel Nate away.

Dorothy turned to Lucie. "Are you coming right home?"

"I have to go pick up Zoë from her job at DQ and then I'll head home," Lucie said, her uneasiness over Zoë returning, a twisting in her stomach. *Lord, please give Mom the words to help Zoë.*

"Tell Zoë I'm looking forward to seeing her." Dorothy touched Lucie's arm and then departed.

The hot wind that had blown all day had finally

given way to an evening breeze. Just the two of them remained—just she and Tanner. His tanned neck glowed with health against the white of his clerical collar. As she watched, he tugged the stiff collar free. The casual gesture sent warm currents flowing through her. *Get a grip, Lucie!*

"Can you give me a lift to DQ?" he asked. "I didn't have time for supper. I'll grab a burger there and then you can drop me at the parsonage on your way back through town."

Lucie hesitated. "Sure." Lucie motioned toward the Bomb, parked under the towering maples. "Climb in."

Lucie backed out of her parking spot and drove to the edge of the now-nearly empty town. She hoped he hadn't noticed her reluctance to be alone with him. *It's just because we're together all the time.*

"I really like your mother," Tanner said.

Of course, you do. She's just your kind of woman— the perfect pastor's wife. Lucie scolded herself for her sour grapes reaction. So Tanner liked her mother on sight and Lucie wasn't like her mother. That didn't mean anything. Because she wasn't going to live the life her mother had. And that was why Tanner Bond, pastor, was totally off-limits to her. "I like her, too," Lucie finally responded.

"That took you a while to spit out. I watched your mother tonight. It's obvious that's she's a caring and sensitive person. What could you possibly have against her?"

"I don't have anything against my mother," Lucie snapped, miffed with herself and irritated with him that he'd noticed her mixed feelings. "I just don't want to *be* my mother."

"What does that mean?"

"Nothing." Lucie regretted letting these words slip through her lips. She hadn't wanted to reveal so much, especially to Tanner. *Sorry, Lord. I'm too old to resurrect these old irritations. I know You love me just the way I am, and so does my mom. And You know I love her, too.*

Tanner looked at her as though measuring her.

She ignored it and clicked on the radio. A weather report predicting rain later filled the silence that yawned between them. *Pastor, I'm getting you home ASAP!*

Lucie parked next to the DQ and got out with Tanner, relieved that they wouldn't be alone in the car on the way home. Even Zoë's company would be welcome. At the window, she let him give his order while she looked through the glass panes trying to locate Zoë.

Finally she asked the red-haired girl at the window, "Will you tell Zoë for me that I'm here to take her home?"

"Zoë left work early," the redhead said, eyeing Lucie warily.

"Left early?" Lucie didn't get it. "How did she get home? Did she call Sophie?"

"I don't know nothing about it," the same girl said in an unconvincing voice.

Lucie stared in at the collection of teens taking orders and swirling cones. In spite of their duties, every one of them was watching her as though waiting for something. "Won't anyone tell me what's going on? Did she go off with…someone?" Lucie ended lamely. *Please, Lord, don't tell me she's run off with Riel Wilkins!*

"You mean Riel?" another girl with a long dark ponytail said. Then with a sly taunt in her tone, she added, "I don't *think* so."

"Don't be catty," the redhead said. "You don't know what happened."

"Whatever." With a lift of her shoulders, the second teen, swishing her ponytail, walked into the back of the DQ.

Nonplussed, Lucie turned to Tanner, not caring about the many eyes and ears trained on her. *Go ahead and gossip about Zoë. I have to find her!*

Tanner was paying for his hamburger and fries. He must have read the concern on her face.

"Why don't you ask to talk to the manager?" he suggested.

"Good idea." Lucie leaned in the order window. "Is the manager here?"

The teen who'd waited on Tanner said, "The assistant manager. Go around back and I'll tell him you're at the employees' entrance."

With a sinking sensation, Lucie, with Tanner beside

her, followed these instructions. *Dear Lord, what's she done now?* Had her mother arrived too late to help with Zoë?

The assistant manager, a young man, met them at the back door. "You asked about Zoë?"

"Yes." Lucie squared her shoulders.

"Well, she was supposed to work till closing tonight. But on her break, she made a phone call. When she hung up, she was real upset. Then that Riel Wilkins stopped by. I was in the back so I didn't hear what was said, but they had a big fight right at the window. I came out and told him that this was a place of business, to get lost. He yelled that leaving was exactly what he was doing...." The young man lifted a shoulder. "And he left."

Lucie tried to read the young manager's face while searching his words for a hidden meaning. "How did Zoë take this?"

His shoulder went up again. "Zoë walked out. I called after her I could fire her for leaving like that. But she was too upset to listen to me." The shoulder rose again. "That's all I know."

His words struck Lucie as ominous. Her shoulders slumped. "Thanks."

The young man nodded with seeming sympathy and went back inside, shutting the door behind him.

"You're worried," Tanner said.

"That's an understatement." Lucie tried to think. Images from her encounter with Riel on that awful night went through her mind. Riel's manhandling of

Zoë still made her angry. What had happened now? A lover's quarrel? "I have to find Zoë and bring her home. Sophie doesn't need this kid acting up now. She's had enough to contend with. And I'm worried about Zoë."

"Well, Zoë doesn't have a car," Tanner observed. "She couldn't go too far on foot."

"Good point. Let's go." Lucie began running to her car.

Clutching his white sack and tall covered soda, Tanner caught up with her. "Where are you going to look?"

If that wasn't just like him, asking the obvious. "Where do you think?" She got in the driver's seat.

Tanner climbed in beside her. "Well, we know she started from here. That way's home." He pointed to the right.

"I know that." Lucie pulled out of the parking lot onto the state highway—and turned left.

"Why are we driving in this direction?" he asked.

"Because if she wanted to go home," Lucie explained, unable to keep the sarcasm out of her tone, "she'd have just called for a ride or walked to the town park. She knew we'd all be there."

Tanner's empty stomach rumbled and he unwrapped the top of his burger and took a bite. "Makes sense."

Gripping the steering wheel with both hands, Lucie drove down the road.

Tanner watched her. To him, it looked like she was overreacting. But maybe he didn't have all the facts.

Lucie had been tight-lipped and worried over more than just Nate. As he chewed his salty fries and swallowed, his mind was all too aware of Lucie's slender, tanned limbs beside him on the car seat. Over the past week, he's wakened every morning with Lucie on his mind.

Whenever he closed his eyes, images of her—the elegant swing of her body as she pitched a softball, the way her whole face lifted and crinkled with amusement, the lilt of her laughter. Stop. He blocked these out of his mind. She didn't have to tell him he was not her type.

Turning his thoughts to Zoë, he looked at Lucie in the low light. "Is there more to this than you've told me?"

She gave him a guarded glance.

Suddenly her reticence irritated him. "Do you trust me by now or not?"

She squirmed in her seat and then sighed.

"Well?" he insisted.

"You know that Zoë's been mixed up with Riel Wilkins, right?" she began cautiously.

"Yes. The deputy mentioned that the first night we came to DQ. And I agreed with his opinion of Riel. Our paths never crossed, but it's generally known that he's a troubled young man from a troubled family."

Lucie sighed again, much louder this time. "Well, I think Zoë and Riel have exchanged more than greetings."

Her words carried more than their surface meaning,

but he didn't want to delve any deeper. Somehow he
hoped Lucie was wrong. "I don't know exactly what
you mean, but I hope Zoë comes to her senses soon.
A year ago, I would have said she was much too sweet
and shy to catch the interest of someone like Riel."

"Riel is a bottom-feeder."

"What?" Her cryptic comment stumped him.

"Riel's low. He's a predator. He looks for girls who
are easy prey. I think Nate's accident must have stirred
up Zoë's fears of being left alone. I mean, her parents
have only been gone…what? Two years? And now
Nate nearly gets killed."

"That's been obvious enough even for me to see,"
he commented dryly. "Is this what was bothering you
and you wouldn't tell me?"

She paused.

He watched her bite her lower lip, that lower lip
that too often enticed him….

"All right. I caught him sneaking her out of the
house off to a deserted spot one night a few weeks
ago."

"Oh." The news hit him like a punch in his midsection. Pretty little Zoë. From church records, he
knew she'd attended St. Andrew's since she was a
baby. Did her big brother know? Tanner hated to think
what this news would do to Nate if he heard about it.

"I bet he'd never have tried something like that
with Nate around," Lucie said, sounding angry.
"Riel's a low life. You see what I mean?"

"All too clearly." Tanner thought of a few other words for Riel. "I wish you'd told me earlier."

"What could you have done?"

"I'm not *that* useless. I would have said something to Riel."

"I think the moment for warning him away had passed before I caught them the other night. Zoë thinks she's in love with him."

He chewed on this briefly. "You're probably right—unfortunately."

"Can you think of any place Zoë or a kid from around here would walk to? Some place that would draw them?"

"Sorry." He munched his burger and stuffed in a few fries, barely tasting them. He knew that Zoë's plight should take his mind off food, but he hadn't eaten since before noon and he needed fuel to deal with this emergency. "Let's leave the highway. Friends would see her on the highway and offer her a ride. If Zoë was upset by something, maybe she wanted to be away from prying eyes and questions."

Lucie glanced at him. "Good idea!" She did a U-turn and sped back to a side road they'd just passed.

Tanner clutched his tall soda, feeling the centrifugal force swirling the ice cubes. "Watch it!"

"Relax. I looked first. No traffic." She careened onto the county road.

"Slow down."

She had the nerve to grin at him. "I'll watch the odometer and only go about two or three miles down this road and then do the same with the other roads we passed. I doubt she'd have gone farther than that. She wouldn't be power-walking. That way we can check each of the roads around the DQ that she might have headed down.''

''Good idea!'' He mimicked Lucie and then drew in a swallow of the sweet cola.

While he finished his high-cholesterol supper, Lucie drove them up and down several country roads. He watched the bronze sun lower itself to the purpled horizon and tried to keep his mind on finding Zoë. But Lucie—as usual—distracted him.

No woman had ever disturbed him, shaken him up like Lucie could. When they'd first met, he'd written her off as flighty. But he'd found out that she was anything but that.

Then he'd admitted to himself that part of the reason Lucie irritated him was that she had a touch of his mother's flamboyance. Many times Lucie's impulsiveness had brought his mother to mind.

His free-spirited mother had even changed her name from her given one, Mary, to Vita, which meant life. Mary had been too stuffy, too insipid a name for his mother. Personally, he thought Mary was a beautiful name with a deep spiritual significance. His mother's rejection of her own name had, to him, summed up her attitude toward her family's religious heritage.

How could Lucie disparage her mother? Lucie's mom hadn't changed her name. She was Dorothy and looked happy to be.

"The silence is getting to me," Lucie said. "Penny for your thoughts."

He studied her. What would she say if he told her what he'd just been thinking? *I don't think so.* "Why don't you want to be like your mother?" he asked instead.

"I'm sorry I brought that up." She sounded displeased with herself. "It was childish. I count myself blessed that I have the mother and father that I have. They truly love each other and have worked side by side for nearly forty years."

He snorted. "You are lucky. My mom has been married three times and is about to marry number four." He sucked in breath. He hadn't meant to say that, but Lucie's words had pulled it out of him.

They bumped over railroad tracks. He glanced both ways out of habit. Movement down the track caught his attention. "Stop." He pointed out his window. "Is that Zoë?"

Chapter Ten

Lucie stopped the car and got out. In the distance, she also noted movement. She nearly called out and then she closed her mouth. The slender form in a white blouse, barely visible in the failing light of day, filled her with a sense of deep sadness, but even more than sadness—dread.

Tanner slid from the passenger side and shut his door quietly, as though aware of Lucie's mood. "What's wrong? I thought you'd call to her."

"I'm afraid I'll spook her and she'll start running. We haven't been getting along that well since I made her come home that night." Lucie couldn't communicate all she was feeling. But she was suddenly frightened for Zoë. "Would you call her?" She glanced at him in the long eerie shadows.

"Hmmm. All right." He stepped around the car,

making himself visible in the glow from the head-lights. "Zoë! Zoë! We've come to take you home."

Lucie felt the prompting to pray. *Lord, bless Zoë in this moment. Whatever has happened, please let Tanner and me help her.*

The figure straggling along the railroad tracks halted and turned toward Tanner. But she didn't move forward.

"Zoë, come on," Tanner coaxed, as though urging a frightened child. "We've come to take you home. It's nearly dark. You shouldn't be out here alone."

Lucie prayed that Zoë would come, not run away and make them chase her on foot.

Zoë started approaching them and her posture spoke volumes. She walked with her head down, visibly dejected.

Lucie prayed for the right words to comfort Zoë. She and Riel must have had a fight. Maybe he'd dumped Zoë for another girl. Lucie mentally berated the jerk. Zoë was too special to be treated like this and to stand for it, too.

Zoë reached them and stopped. She stared at them.

"What is it?" Tanner asked softly.

"I'm pregnant." Zoë launched the words at them, both fearful and daring at the same time.

A shock wave shuddered through Lucie. She clamped her mouth shut, not wanting to say the wrong thing. Pregnant? A baby? No wonder Riel had fought with her. He wouldn't take to fatherhood well.

Tanner held out his arm to Zoë. "Come on. We'll take you home and we'll sort this out."

"A baby can't be sorted out," Zoë declared tearfully, folding her arms in front of her. "I'm going to have a baby and Riel is leaving for the marines tomorrow."

Lucie heard herself gasp. "What?"

"Come here, Zoë," Tanner urged.

"He said no one was going to tie him down with a kid." Zoë spat out the words.

"Oh, Zoë!" Lucie rushed to her and wrapped the girl in her arms. "I'm so sorry. How could he?"

Zoë didn't pull away, but she didn't return Lucie's embrace. She just stood there, stiff and still. "The sheriff told his parents that Riel is the one who stole those trucks last spring and took them for joyrides. I don't know how he knew it was true, but it was. I know it was. I was with Riel." Zoë began to cry aloud. "I've been so stupid." The girl leaned into Lucie, who held her close.

Lucie tried to absorb these facts and all their implications.

"The sheriff told Riel's dad," Zoë continued, trying to control her weeping, "that either he signed Riel up for the service or the sheriff would begin trying to collect enough evidence to try Riel for the joyriding. He didn't know if he had enough to convict Riel, but he'd try to get enough to charge him."

Lucie realized that Zoë's nerves had taken over and the girl was just spilling everything that she'd been holding in for months. Lucie patted the girl's back as she shook with weeping.

"But the sheriff said he'd rather see Riel in boot camp than prison. It might straighten him out. At first, Riel told his dad that he wouldn't enlist. He'd let the sheriff try to make a case against him." Zoë swallowed, again trying to pull herself together. "But when I told him I was pregnant...he called me names...he said I was trying to trap him with a baby." Zoë moaned, her distress too deep for words.

Lucie hugged Zoë tighter, absorbing the girl's trembling. Lucie could only pray. *Dear God. Dear God.* She motioned Tanner to come closer.

He approached them and helped Lucie tuck the girl into the back seat of the car. Then Tanner took his place in the passenger seat and Lucie got in and turned the car around. She and Tanner exchanged glances.

At first, Lucie was at a loss for words. Then she said, "Zoë, Riel doesn't deserve you." Again, she recalled Riel's rough treatment of Zoë.

"I loved him. He said he loved me." Zoë's voice shook with emotion and half-swallowed sobs. "What did I do wrong? He said I wouldn't get pregnant. He'd take care of it. I didn't mean to get pregnant."

"Stop it, Zoë." Lucie spoke up, her heart aching for the girl. "You didn't do anything that would make you deserve being treated so poorly by someone you trusted. You are not the one who engineered this situation. Riel did. Whatever protection he used, he knew there was still a chance you'd get pregnant."

"It's all my fault," Zoë keened. "I knew it was wrong."

"No, it isn't all your fault." Tanner sounded very certain. "Riel is shirking his responsibility to the baby and you. And you don't deserve such treatment. You did something wrong, but this isn't the end of the world."

"Everyone will know! I just want to die." Zoë's voice became a wail.

"Zoë, don't talk like that!" Lucie declared, frightened of what the teenager might do. "You aren't alone. You have family."

"You will have to face this, Zoë," Tanner said, "but Riel is the real loser. You are a lovely young woman with a heart capable of deep love. Riel is a fool to leave you. Any man would be fortunate to be loved by you."

Zoë's weeping ebbed. "Do you think so?"

Lucie realized she'd been clutching the steering wheel. She relaxed her grip and let herself get more comfortable. Tanner's words had tempered the despondent atmosphere in the car. She thanked heaven he'd come along tonight.

"I know so," Tanner insisted. "Now we're going to take you home and you must trust us—your friends and family—to help you through this. You've done wrong, but God's forgiveness can cover any mistake. The important thing now is to take care of yourself and have a healthy baby."

"I don't know if I can do this—"

"You will do what you have to," Tanner said. "Your baby is counting on you."

Tanner's words continued to impress Lucie. He'd said just the right thing. Zoë still wept, but the edge of hysteria had gone.

Lucie drove through the deserted town, listening to Zoë weep with what sounded like fatigue and worry. Finally home glowed ahead, light pouring from its large windows, drawing them.

Lucie and Tanner walked on either side of Zoë toward the house. How would they break the news to Sophie and Nate? *Oh, Lord, I'm so glad Mom's here.*

The back door opened and Dorothy came out and stood under the yellow porch light.

"Aunt Dorothy!" Zoë called out. "Aunt Dorothy!"

Lucie's mom opened her arms and Zoë ran to her.

Relieved, Lucie halted beside Tanner and watched Dorothy comfort Zoë and draw her inside.

"I take it that means Zoë knows your mom?" Tanner asked.

Lucie nodded, suddenly able to take a deep breath. "Yes, my parents unofficially adopted her as a niece when she came to live with Nate and Sophie."

"I like your mom."

Lucie looked at him, the urge to hug him again overcame her, and this time, she didn't repress it. She threw her arms around him. He smelled of french fries, clean soap and the scent that was his alone. "I do, too, and I'm so glad she came tonight."

After a moment's hesitation, he returned her embrace, then he released her. He looked skyward. "God's timing is always the best."

Two weeks later, Lucie sat beside Tanner and the rest of the extended family at the long maple table in Nate and Sophie's dining room. Mrs. Hazelton had brought over a full meal, including a luscious-looking coconut cream pie. And everyone had decided to eat a bit earlier than the usual supper hour while everything was still hot. Lucie had suppressed a burst of excitement when Tanner had chosen the seat beside her.

Lucie looked around the table, from face to face— her mother, Zoë, Sophie, Nate, the boys and Carly in her high chair. Lucie had only been in Pleasant Prairie since late May, just about two months. Things had definitely improved since her arrival. The softball games—mornings and Thursday evenings—continued to draw support and bring the locals and the newcomers into friendly contact.

Thanks to Ignacio and Tanner, Nate was home from the hospital and would soon put the wheelchair away and stick to his crutches. Sam Torres was working weekends at the farm. Riel Wilkins had left town and Zoë was behaving more like herself again. A trip to the doctor had verified she was over two months pregnant, and both she and the baby appeared healthy. Nate and Sophie took the news well though privately, Sophie had commented to Lucie that it never rained, it always poured.

Lucie was wisely leaving Zoë up to her mother.

Lucie had no experience with teenagers expecting babies. However, after years in the ministry with her father, her mother had had plenty. So much had been accomplished in such a short time!

Still, one other matter still nagged Lucie. She hoped Tanner wouldn't be upset with her when he found out what she started. And she'd better prepare him, lead up to it some way. But exactly how? He was such a worrywart. But a sweet worrywart.

"I wish Ignacio were here," Lucie said as she spooned a generous portion of the layered casserole of ground beef, green beans, corn, water chestnuts and chow mein noodle topping. "This looks *de-lish*." Ignacio would have been a good ally when she broke the news of her latest action to Tanner.

"Ignacio is having supper with Sammie's family tonight." Danny spoke up. "I think he wants to see if Sammie's dad will take Fella back."

Upon hearing his name, Fella sat up in the kitchen doorway and barked. Not to be outdone, Sancho got up and yipped.

"Down, boys," Nate said, chuckling.

Lucie remember all too well Sam Torres's reaction when she'd try to give Fella back to him back in May. But Sam had come to the ballpark to watch his son and he'd proven to be Nate's right hand on the farm. She had yet to see a smile on Sam, however. "I'm kinda getting used to having Fella around."

"Me, too." Danny forked up some of the casserole. "But Sammie still wants Fella back. He told me so."

"I like Fella here," Mikey countered, swinging his legs and bumping the table leg.

"Mikey, settle those legs down," Sophie admonished. "Fella is welcome to stay or welcome to go back to Sammie. We will still love him either way."

Lucie sighed. In spite of everything, Sophie was almost back to normal. Her distress had subsided markedly since Nate came home. Even the trips back and forth for physical and occupational therapy didn't frazzle her.

"Honey," Sophie said, "I saw Harry at the feed store today and he said he might be able to help Sam out with the harvest."

Nate gave a dry laugh. "That's what Harry always says. But he's never been free to help me in the past. Always pulls a muscle or something else. Come fall, he'll have more excuses than a dog has fleas. We won't think about the harvest now. I got most of the crop in before the accident. Sam is taking of things for now. We'll get the crops out of the fields someway. I might even be well enough to work by fall."

Sophie didn't look convinced, but she smiled and nodded. "Sure."

Lucie tried to decide if she should spring her news on Tanner in front of everyone or do it privately. *Decisions, decisions.*

The phone rang in the kitchen. Lucie got up and ran to pick it up. "Hello?"

"Hey, pumpkin, it's your dad."

Lucie grinned. "Hi, Dad."

"Is your mother free?"

"We're eating supper early, but I'll call her. Mom!" She turned to find her mother right behind her. She handed her the phone and went back to the dining room table.

Lucie took a bite of the tasty casserole and chewed it. Of course, Tanner would be irritated with her at first, but he'd come around. He always did. *He should be used to me by now!*

Dorothy returned to the table. "I told Tom that I'd call him back after the meal."

"What did he want?" Lucie asked.

"Just something that's come up at the church. He wanted to get the feminine viewpoint from me."

This was a new idea for Lucie. She didn't remember her father asking for her mother's opinion very often as Lucie was growing up. Had he just begun this or had he done it all along and Lucie just hadn't noticed? Lucie studied her mother in this new light.

The meal proceeded with the usual spilled milk and discussions over whether water chestnuts came from trees—the usual evidence of children at the table. After Lucie cut the pie, everyone scattered with things to do. Leaving Sophie wiping Carly's hands and face clean, Lucie and Tanner took their plates of coconut cream pie out onto the back porch. Lucie heard her mother at the kitchen phone, dialing her father. The boys were throwing a ball to Fella. Sancho ran along with Fella, yipping with excitement.

Against this backdrop of happy sounds, Lucie tingled at having Tanner right beside her.

Lounging against the railing, Tanner scooped up some of the fluffy cream-colored pie into his mouth. Whipped cream dotted his lip.

Lucie traced the spot with the tip of her little finger and felt suddenly breathless. "Messy."

"So what's up?" he said, looking sideways at her.

"What do you mean?" she asked archly, licking her fingers and feeling ripples of awareness.

"You stared at me so much during dinner that I kept looking down to see what I had spilled on my shirt." He gave her a half grin. "I hadn't spilled anything. That tells me you want me to do something. What?"

Deciding to make him coax it out of her, Lucie dipped her fork into her piece of pie and glanced down at the floor. Tanner's tanned feet in sandals caught her eye. How did he do it? The man even had cute toes!

"Lucie, what is it?" Tanner asked in a suspicious tone. "What are you plotting to get me to do?"

"Well." She let the light sweet cream melt on her tongue. "I was thinking we need to do something more—for the newcomers." She licked her spoon and dipped it into the creamy custard. "I mean, we have them coming to the games on Thursday evenings and the two groups are beginning to greet each other. But…"

"But?" Tanner prompted with that same current of wariness.

She savored another sweet spoonful, taunting him with her gaze.

"Lucie."

Well, here goes nothing! "But I think we should be doing more—" Lucie plunged in headfirst "—something to get the newcomers and the locals talking to each other. When you were having those discussions with the church board about what to do to bring the newcomers into the community more, did you actually come up with any plans?"

He cocked an eyebrow at her. "We discussed initiating a Spanish-speaking worship service for Saturday evening or Sunday afternoon. We were going to hire a translator."

"But that would separate people, not bring them together." She waved her spoon. "We need something that brings people together!"

"I agree. But what?"

"Well, I'm glad you asked," Lucie said with a satisfied smile. "I think we need to have an informal social after the next Thursday-night game."

He straightened. "Where did you get that idea?"

"From Miguel's mother." She fluffed the creamy topping with the end of her spoon. "When I stopped by their trailer the other night—"

"Hold it. Hold it." Tanner set his pie down on the porch railing. "Something like this takes planning. We need a host. We'll need to advertise—"

"Well, we better get busy because I've told Maria

that we'll have that social after the next Thursday-night game.''

''What?''

''And I think the parsonage would be the perfect spot for it. Everyone can just walk there after the game.''

''Lucie!'' He upset his dish. His pie splatted on the ground below. Fella and Sancho raced over and devoured the broken crust and creamy filling.

Tanner glared at her.

With a saucy grin, she took his fork and scooped up a generous bite of her pie and aimed it for his mouth.

Still glaring, he accepted the morsel.

''It'll be fun,'' Lucie crooned. ''You'll see.''

Chapter Eleven

After the next Thursday night's game, Lucie stood at the bottom of Tanner's freshly painted gray back steps. The parents—nearly all—had come for refreshments and stood around the uncut lawn or sat in lawn chairs under shade trees. Lucie felt an urgency. That made her feel out of place in this tranquil scene. Time was short and growing shorter. Soon, the mosquitoes would drive everyone home. She needed inspiration for another hint at how to continue knitting this community together. *Lord, You've brought them together here behind the church. Where do we go from here? Lead them. Lead me.*

As she sipped a cold glass of tart lemonade, she eavesdropped on several conversations.

To her right:

"Here's my friend." Danny pulled Miguel over to Sophie. "His name is Miguel."

Sophie leaned down. "Nice to meet you, Miguel. I'm Sophie."

"Hi, Sophie," Miguel said.

"*Hijo,* son," Maria, coming to Miguel's side, interrupted, "please call her Señora Sophie."

Sophie turned and smiled. "You're Miguel's mother? We'd like to have Miguel come over after a morning game…."

To Lucie's left:

"…wish you and Sophie had let us know," Mitch, the mechanic—who was letting Lucie pay off her new muffler at ten dollars a week—was saying to Nate, "that you needed help. Pleasant Prairie always takes care of its own."

"Yeah," Nate added, "I know, Mitch, but our priest and Ignacio just volunteered. On my own, I don't think I would have asked."

"Lucie let us know," Ignacio put in. "And the *padre* and me—we are from Pleasant Prairie also."

About ten spaces in front of Lucie:

"So," Tanner was saying to Juan, "you think the church's mower just needs new spark plugs?"

"Yeah." Juan stood with his hands shoved in his pockets.

"Can you come out tomorrow and take care of that?"

"Sure, man, I mean, *padre*…"

Lucie turned back to the first conversation.

"I wish I knew more about the Bible," Maria told Sophie.

Hearing this cue, Lucie moved forward. The Lord had provided the next step.

After saying the opening prayer, Tanner finally admitted it to himself. Days later, he was still irritated with Lucie. He'd tried to banish anger from his mind without success. It was the first Sunday night in August and he sat at Nate and Sophie's dining room table, his grandfather's worn black leather Bible open in front of him. He'd chosen this Bible for tonight, hoping that remembering his grandfather's faithful service to God would calm him.

The air-conditioning kept the room moderately comfortable; a box fan sat on the floor circulating the air. After spending so many days and nights there, this house had become his second home. He usually felt at ease there.

Not tonight. He gazed around the table at the people who'd shown up for the first home Bible study—the home Bible study that Lucie had invited Maria to—before she'd even discussed it with him. At this thought, he felt the steam rise in him again.

Maria, of course, was here, but more surprising were the others that had joined her—Ignacio, the Hazeltons and Sam Torres's wife. Finally, Nate and Sophie made up the gathering of nine, a good number for a small group.

Sam had come along with his wife, but was out in the barn going over the equipment with the oil can. Sammie and Miguel were outside playing with Mikey and Danny under Zoë's supervision, their yells filtering through the closed windows. Dorothy was in the kitchen preparing iced tea and dessert for them.

"'For the darkness is passing away, and the real light is already shining,'" Sophie read aloud from the First Epistle of John, chapter two.

Maria looked to Tanner. "What is this light and *oscuridad*, I mean, the darkness?"

Tanner burned with aggravation and knew he was wrong to be annoyed with Lucie. He forced himself to focus on the topic at hand. "All through the Bible, light symbolizes God's truth while darkness represents the absence of truth or sin. The worst darkness is being separated from God—the greatest tragedy."

"My dad," Lucie broke in, "always says that the closer you are to God, the more light you have in your life. God brings honesty and truth with him."

Tanner hardened himself against Lucie's buoyancy. He didn't want to get a lift from her ever-present enthusiasm. Hadn't he had enough of his mother's impulsiveness in his childhood—nothing ever certain, everything up for grabs? How was it that Lucie got past his defenses? How did Lucie have the power to get him to do things that weren't natural to him—like playing baseball? And why did he put up with her rushing him into things?

Tanner's conscience answered his own questions. *You always go along with Lucie because somehow she triggers you into action.* Tanner shifted restlessly with this thought.

"I remember your father saying that," Sophie added, Carly on her lap dozing, so completely relaxed, she looked as if she were without any bone structure. "Lucie's dad always said that God's light made us see things clearer. So that if you stay close to God, you could make better decisions."

"How do you do that?" Mort asked.

Lucie reached over and fingered Carly's dark curls. The play of the pale fingers in the dark brown hair captivated Tanner.

And in spite of his inner turmoil, he was thrilled his students weren't just sitting listening to him. Exchanging thoughts and ideas helped students absorb more deeply what was being presented. The Bible study couldn't be going better!

Lord, why can't I get rid of my anger toward Lucie? I don't want to spoil this evening and I don't want to hang on to my resentment. I know it's wrong. Why can't I stop being upset with her?

Tanner looked up to see all eyes on him. He cleared his throat. "One stays closer to God by doing what we are tonight. We are reading His words, which He inspired the apostle John to write."

"'Thy words have I hid in my heart that I might not sin against Thee,'" Nate recited. "My mom taught me that when I was Danny's age."

Sophie smiled at Nate and patted his arm.

Lucie continued to affectionately fluff the sleeping baby's locks of hair.

Tanner couldn't take his eyes from her. He felt the

conflict within him—the pull to this woman who loved
without reservation, and in opposition, his frustration
at her leaping ahead of him, time after time. He made
himself return to the lesson. "Why don't you read on,
Maria?"

"'Whoever says that he is in the light, yet hates his
brother, is in the darkness to this very hour.'" Maria
stopped without being asked. She pursed her lips and
looked at Tanner. "But sometimes you can't help it.
I mean if someone has treated you badly, it's hard not
to hate them. If I hate someone, does that mean that I
am in darkness, separated from God?"

Maria's innocent words were like burning stakes
thrust into Tanner's heart. *God, I am so sorry. Why
am I so angry at Lucie? She was just being herself.*
"That's a difficult question, Maria."

"Not really." Lucie spoke up, her delicate hand
leaving the dark curls. "The Lord's Prayer says, 'Forgive us our sins as we forgive those who sin against
us.' We must forgive because God forgave us. Holding
on to a grudge isn't an option."

Tanner ground his teeth silently. *She's right.* Another more painful idea intruded. *Am I angry at Lucie
or at myself? Am I upset because she moves things
along while I hang back?*

Maria frowned. "I've been holding on to anger
against that boy, the one who left town...' Then she
colored, obviously realizing that she'd brought up a
touchy subject.

The fact that Riel had abandoned Zoë, who was

pregnant with his child, had soon become common knowledge in Pleasant Prairie. Evidently it had even reached Shangri-La. Remembering Zoë that night by the railroad tracks steadied Tanner. *I was able to help Zoë that night. Even Lucie said so.*

"I've been having the same trouble," Nate rumbled.

Tanner didn't blame him.

Dorothy had come into the doorway. "That's only natural, Nate. Riel hurt someone you love." Dorothy walked over to Sophie and held out her arms for the sleeping baby. Sophie stood and settled Carly into Dorothy's arms. "But in the end, Riel lost what he might have gained by staying."

Before Tanner could put his question into words, Mrs. Torres spoke for the first time. "What would he have gained?" The woman sounded curious and unconvinced at the same time, matching Tanner's reaction.

Dorothy turned and smiled at her. "He would have gained a loving family and a precious child."

Bull's-eye. Dorothy's words nailed him. All Tanner could think was *What am I losing by being angry with Lucie?*

Finally, the house was quiet, the children already asleep upstairs, Sancho at the foot of Danny's bed and Fella at Mikey's. It was Tanner's turn to stay overnight with Nate, whom he'd just helped out of the shower and into bed.

In his shorts and T-shirt, Tanner perched on the top step of the back porch, barefoot and with his elbows propped on his knees. A strange mixture of emotions tumbled around inside him. He felt uplifted by the Bible study and it was easy to see why.

Maria had asked if she and Mrs. Torres could bring another lady with them next week. Ignacio had said he'd try to bring another friend of his, too. If the group continued to grow, Tanner would split it into two to make room for more people. That's why Lucie had suggested they begin with a short book like the First Epistle of John, one that could be finished in a month. Who knew how many people might end up growing spiritually, all because of Lucie?

Tanner wanted to tell Lucie how glad he was that she'd gotten the ball rolling the way she had. He had tried and tried to think of a way to get Lucie alone so they could talk, but in vain.

The door behind him opened quietly and bare feet padded toward him. He knew it was Lucie without even turning around. *Do I already recognize her foot-steps?* The disturbing idea sank deep inside him.

"So," she asked from behind him in a pert whisper, "still mad at me?" She plopped down beside him, wearing a pair of cutoffs and a faded T-shirt.

Feeling his neck turn red, he put his head in his hands. "Was I that obvious?"

"To me." She had the nerve to chuckle. "I've had a lot of experience over the past few weeks in making you mad."

More shame. He groaned quietly. "I'm sorry, but you—"

"I get under your skin."

"Exactly." She must have come fresh from the shower. She smelled of some floral shampoo that made him want to lean closer. He restrained himself, but the fragrance went to his head.

"Tanner, I don't think that's going to change," she said wryly. "I think we're just really different people."

"I can agree with that." He straightened up again, trying to resist the spell that her nearness was weaving around and within him.

"I mean, I like to move ahead." She held up one palm and then the other. "While you—"

"I like to think things over and pray about them—" he cut in, unwilling to let her score all the points.

"I pray, too. But I pray differently."

"What do you mean?" He propped his back against the rough railing and contemplated her. She leaned backward, her elbows resting on the top step.

"Each morning I pray that God will direct my path. So when a thought occurs to me, I figure it has God's blessing. Because I already asked Him to guide me through my day."

While enjoying the elegant pose she presented with her slender legs stretching downward, Tanner considered this new idea. "I hadn't thought of it that way. You pray that each morning?"

She nodded.

"I still like to think things over." He clung to his right to be himself. "I don't like rushing around half-cocked."

She nudged him. Her elbow touched his chest. Only thin cotton knit separated her skin from his. Her touch upped his awareness of her warm vibrancy so near, yet not to be touched. "I know you don't. But sometimes you have to seize the moment—carpe diem."

"That's seize the day."

"Same idea. Don't be argumentative."

Her hair brushed just below his chin. He breathed in her scent full force. "Why didn't you take a moment to ask me whether I wanted to host the families after Thursday night's game?" He felt petty saying this, but it was the crux of his anger.

"That was wrong of me." She inched closer to him. "I'm sorry."

Her apology—so unexpected—took the wind out of his sails. "You admit it?" He would have inched away, but the rough wood railing already dug into his back.

"I do." She rested her hand lightly on his forearm.

Her nearness went to his head—intoxicating. "Are you also sorry," he asked archly, a disconcerting smile playing at one corner of his mouth, "about forming a Bible study and volunteering me to teach it?"

"A little. Tanner—" she squeezed his arm "—sometimes things have to be done at the right moment. In both of these cases, I had to move while that special moment existed. And you shouldn't be upset because I didn't include you in the decision, because I had.''

"You had?" What was she trying to put over him? "When? Did I sleep through a conversation with you?"

"When you say something lame like that, it sounds as if you did." She bumped her shoulder into his as though trying to shake him up. "You let me know almost at our first meeting that you wanted to bring the newcomers into this community and that you had been praying that God would help you accomplish this. Have I done anything that resulted in setting this goal—your main goal—back?"

He hadn't thought of that. "No." He finally understood her reasoning. He didn't like it, but he got it.

"Did it ever occur to you that God may have brought me here to get the ball rolling and keep it rolling?"

"Because I couldn't?" he asked, feeling his feathers ruffling all over again. He didn't like his reaction. It spoke of stubborn pride.

She punched him again. "Ever read First Corinthians about the different parts of the body of Christ? Well, I'm the sassy part."

Her unaffected, completely honest words bowled him over. He couldn't help himself, he laughed. "I don't remember that part being listed."

"Well, St. Paul hadn't met me personally."

"Oh?" He faced her in the moonlight. *This woman is going to drive me crazy.* "I'm sorry." The words came easily, but he realized he meant it. She was right. He'd made his goal clear. And with a live-wire like

Lucie that evidently was all that was necessary to get her started taking action. *I'm sorry, Lord. Forgive me. Thank You for sending Lucie.*

A cicada shrieked higher, higher, distracting him. The corn in the nearby field was rustling, audibly growing. When he was new in town, he'd thought the farmer who'd told him he'd be able to hear corn grow was pulling the new city preacher's leg. Now he recognized the sound. Harvest wouldn't be late this year. The crops had gone in early. He would have to do something about Nate's crops.

The warm, enticing woman next to him leaned closer. "You need to have some faith in me and in God."

"I have faith in God—"

"Sometimes you don't act like it."

He fought the spurt of irritation this caused. "Don't question my faith in God. I'm just a cautious person. And I guess I just don't like being rushed."

"I'm the same way—"

"What?" *Lucie, you're always in a rush.*

"I mean, I don't like being told what to do, either. And I don't mean to do that to you. It's just…"

"What?"

"It's just that when the way looks so clear to me and I sense the moment has come to act, I can't hold back!"

"The moment has come," echoed in his mind. "I don't want you to."

"Did I hear right?" She leaned close to his face, grinning that cheeky grin of hers.

The moment has come. Tanner kissed her.

Chapter Twelve

Lucie held her breath, mesmerized by Tanner's soft, persuasive lips and the prickle of new beard starting on his chin. Who had taught him to kiss like this? She let herself ease closer to him. Extending her arms until they rested on his shoulders, she crossed her wrists behind his neck. "Tanner," she sighed against his mouth.

She realized that she'd closed her eyes and she opened them. Tanner's dark eyelashes fanned across his high, smooth cheekbones. He looked completely absorbed in the business of kissing her. She smiled and pulled her lips away.

His eyes flew open. "Lucie?"

She chuckled low in her throat. And began her own kiss.

Warm air rushed past her lips as he groaned, tilting his chin downward and giving her the best angle. He

kissed her as if it were the most natural thing to do—
as if he'd been kissing her for years.

Finally, she pulled her mouth from his and settled
her cheek on his firm shoulder. "Well."

Dazed by his own initiative, Tanner cradled her,
linking both arms around her. The night breeze played
with her moist curls, causing them to tickle his chin.
He hugged her closer, sinking his face into the fragrant
curve between her shoulder and neck. "Well."

He didn't need words now. He just needed Lucie in
his arms.

She turned her face up to his again and smiled at
him.

His heart melted at the warmth in her gaze.

"So, here we are," she whispered, "kissing on Sophie's back porch."

To prove her right, he lifted her head with one hand
and moved his lips over hers again. *I'm kissing Lucie.
And nothing has ever felt so right.*

His conscious mind wanted to barge in and make
sense of the moment, but he stopped it—with another
kiss. He wanted to go on kissing Lucie. On and on.

She pulled away and laid her head on his shoulder
again. "I didn't even know I wanted you to kiss me.
Is that crazy or what?" she murmured, her lips grazing
the tender skin of his neck.

He chuckled. "Had me fooled, too."

"I guess this is something we need to…" She
groped for words in vain. "No need to rush, right?"

"We have all the time in the world." He said the

words, but knew they weren't factual. Lucie didn't live in Pleasant Prairie, but he did. And they weren't at all alike....

He halted this line of thought. He didn't want to let reality enter the moment, this wonderful spontaneous moment. After all, that's what Lucie did best, right? Wonderful, spontaneous moments.

He tugged her closer and she came freely just as he hoped she would, nestling close to him. Breathing in her fragrance, he kissed the top of her head, feeling her silken hair springing wet against his lips. *Lord, tomorrow help me make sense of this. I didn't expect this... But right now, just let me savor...kissing Lucie.*

Lucie couldn't get last night out of her mind. Who knew stick-in-the-mud Tanner Bond—clerical collar and all—could kiss like that? *Wow!*

August afternoon sun blazed down on Lucie's cloth garden hat. She and her mother were picking the first of the corn and last of the green beans for supper. And tomatoes and green peppers for salad. Lucie glanced over her shoulder at the back porch, trying to make what had happened there last night feel real.

"You planted an excellent garden, dear," her mother said as she twisted tender young ears of corn off the six-foot-plus cornstalks.

Lucie had insisted on doing the bending job of picking clean the bush green beans. "You mean I planted an excellent small farm." Thinking of Tanner's kisses brought a rosy warmth to her face. She hid this from her mother by keeping her head down.

Also wearing a hat, a wide-brimmed straw, Dorothy said, "Well, Sophie has become a true farmer's wife, and her garden shows that."

What would Mom think of me kissing Tanner? "Sophie said Dad called yesterday. How's he doing?"

Dorothy chuckled. "He misses my cooking. Anna has been trying out new recipes on him and he's had a bit more variety in his diet than he's accustomed to. And he asked for advice on the fall children's Sunday school materials. I would be ordering them if I were home."

"He depends on you a lot. Everyone does." Lucie put into words what troubled her most about her mother's life. This reminded her that kissing Tanner, a clergyman, was dangerous for her. "Doesn't that bother you sometimes?"

"Not really. After getting married and having children, I just got used to being depended on—"

"But sometimes people take advantage of you." Lucie shoved two handfuls of green beans into the garden basket on the ground beside her. While Lucie's lips were on Tanner's last night, where had her head been?

"It may look like that, Lucie, but believe me, I know when to say no. I didn't always understand that, but your father and I made a pact when we got married that our first job was loving each other and our children. Those were the first jobs that God had called us to. If we did them right, the church business would go only better.''

Lucie mulled this over. Had Tanner ever thought about these priorities? Cicadas shrieked and brown grasshoppers bounced around her. As she recalled her childhood, she realized that what mother had said was true. That was until her teen years. Before then, she had always felt secure in her parents' love. Why had that changed when she was in her teens? Had her rebellion pushed her parents away? After dealing with Zoë, this was a painful thought, too painful. She switched topics.

''How's Zoë doing?'' Lucie lowered her voice.

Dorothy gave a long sigh. ''Poor child, she's going to have to grow up a lot this year.''

''Has she decided what to do about the baby?'' At twenty-three, Lucie didn't feel ready for motherhood. How would Zoë handle it?

''Not yet.'' Dorothy tossed ears of corn, one by one into the bushel by her feet—thump, thump. ''We've discussed adoption and what she'll face if she keeps the baby. It will be painful because Riel will be no help—''

''He'll still have to support the baby,'' Lucie said with a pugnacious burst.

''Sometimes it's best to let sleeping dogs lie,'' Dorothy replied. ''He's not the kind of person Zoë wants in her life or her baby's.''

''I wish she could have realized that before,'' Lucie

couldn't stop herself from snapping. She'd at least tried to talk sense to Zoë.

"She was terrified of losing her brother, of being left all alone. Riel sensed that and played on it for his own purposes. He—or really, his lies about loving her forever, and of just the two of them against the world—made her feel secure."

"But they were just lies. Why didn't she see that? Why wouldn't she listen?"

"Unfortunately, that's very common. When people are in the middle of crises and making bad decisions, they don't listen. The fear or the anger speaks too loudly, overriding everything else."

Under her thin T-shirt, a bead of sweat trickled down Lucie's bent back. She thought about the recent Bible lesson, about her father's wisdom that staying close to God helped you make wiser decisions. One decision she'd made long ago was that she never wanted to be her mother, or more exactly, be a minister's wife. Had that been a wise decision? It had seemed so, but was it really etched in stone? Could she change her mind? Tanner's kiss rushed through her like hot summer wind, jarring her preconceptions loose.

Had she decided to kiss Tanner Bond last night? Or had she merely allowed herself to be swept away on the thrill of Tanner's kisses? Had that been a good decision? Did she and Tanner have a future, or had they just shared a kiss on Sophie's back porch?

Row by row, Lucie swished her hands over the low

green bean plants, making sure she hadn't missed any beans. She let herself concentrate on the mundane task, pushing away her inner conflict. Finally she said, "I'm just so glad that you came, Mom."

A pause.

Lucie looked up. Dorothy was staring at her.

"What's wrong?"

Dorothy turned back to the cornstalks. "It's just been a while since you've sounded so happy to see me."

That gave Lucie pause. She straightened, her garden basket in hand. "I'm sorry that you've thought I didn't want you around. I've just been so busy getting through school—"

"I think it's time I said I'm sorry." Dorothy didn't turn around, but held to her picking. "I've regretted being so hard on you when you were in high school."

Lucie swallowed a lump that had come into her throat. Zoë's rebellion was unpleasantly fresh in her mind. Had she ever acted like Nate's sister? "I was— I was a bit of a rebel—"

"Well, you were very different from your sisters, I'll give you that." Her mom's tone was light, almost teasing. "They didn't push against the limits I'd set like you did."

"I can't help it. That's my nature." Lucie moved to the tomato plant and began twisting plump, ripe-red ones from the vines. A trace of her old feeling of rejection reared up. *Lord, I want to leave this behind me. I love my mom. You know that!*

"I know and love you just the way you are, Lucie. It's just that your teen years came at just the wrong time."

Lucie heard her mother dragging the bushel of corn to the end of the row. "What do you mean?" She tried to keep her tone from sounding accusing. "I didn't have much control over turning thirteen."

Dorothy sighed. "Right when you wanted to wear ragged blue jeans to worship on Sunday morning and pierce your ears more than the usual, your father was having trouble with some of the board members at church." Dorothy brought a handful of glossy green peppers and let them fall into another garden basket near Lucie. "I shouldn't have internalized their criticism of your father and then taken it out on you. I was afraid they'd use your youthful rebellion as a weapon against him. It was a lack of faith on my part."

These words were a revelation. Lucie stood up. "Why didn't you tell me what was going on?"

Her mother glanced up from the pepper plants, but kept picking. "I didn't…your father didn't…want you girls to be aware of the behind-the-scenes squabbling in the church leadership. He said it would be bad for you at your stage of Christian maturity."

"Why?" Lucie felt her heart being drawn upward. Finally, she understood what had gone so very wrong between her and her mom, whom she'd always loved but whom she'd felt separated from.

"Because there will always be someone at church

who causes trouble. That just comes with the job, especially at a large church where there are many successful people. Not everyone who attends church or sits on a church board is a consistent Christian. Some are just playing a part. Some have a long way to go toward being a mature Christian. So there are bumps in the road. That's the best way I can explain it.''

"I know that. Dad explained that to me." Lucie recalled his telling her this more than once when she'd pointed out un-Christian behavior in a church member.

Dorothy took a hanky from her pocket and wiped the perspiration—and maybe tears?—from her face. "Well, your father didn't want you to have to deal with that when you were already restless under any authority. But unfortunately, I let their criticism get under my skin and our relationship suffered for it. Can you forgive me?''

Stepping wide over garden rows, she hurried to her mother. She threw her arms around Dorothy and hugged her, her hat falling to the ground.

Mom hugged her back. "Oh, Lucie, my sweet daughter."

Lucie felt her mother's unconditional love for her seep deep inside, layer by layer, a healing warmth. "I'm sorry, Mom."

"Don't be sorry, dear. You were the child. I was the parent. I knew better, but I let worry cause trouble between us. The fault was mine, not yours. I'm just so glad that you called me to come when you needed me. That meant everything to me."

Lucie hugged her mother tighter. "I'm so glad I had you to call."

Sophie burst out of the back door. "Lucie! Lucie! Tanner's on the phone for you!"

At the sound of his name, Lucie's heart lifted. *Tanner!*

"It's bad news!"

After supper that night, Lucie pulled into the church parking lot and jumped out of the Bomb. Tanner was waiting for her behind the screen door of the parsonage. She hurried toward him. "I can't believe it!"

"I'm not thrilled, either." Tanner's hands were stuffed into his pockets. He pulled out one and opened the door for her.

She walked into the air-conditioned room, wishing she could hug him. He looked like he needed a hug. "Everything we've worked for all summer—it can't just be over." When she thought of the kids from the trailer court and the friends they'd made in town, she felt like bursting into tears.

"Ignacio called me when his daughter called him from work with the news. The layoffs will start in two weeks."

"It's a done deal? The packing plant really has been sold to a conglomerate?" Now *she* needed a hug from Tanner.

"Yes, at first, the employees thought this was good news, that they'd get more work—"

"But?" Lucie cut in.

"But it turns out the conglomerate just bought it for the equipment. They will start laying people off, several at a time, a week after Labor Day, and will have everything moved out before Thanksgiving."

Lucie groaned. "Maria and so many others came not just because of jobs, but for the schools here."

"I know. I just feel so…angry." Tanner raked his hands through his hair.

His tone made her examine him more closely. Tanner didn't look like himself. He looked edgy and out of sorts. Remembering how many times in the past he'd put off supper, Lucie peered around the red-and-white kitchen where they stood. "Haven't you eaten yet? Or did you just clean up?"

"I've been busy with my sermon notes and the next Bible study lesson. I wasn't in the mood to eat."

Lucie opened his refrigerator door and glimpsed a package of hot dogs, a half loaf of bread and a jar of pickles. He'd been eating with her family so much, he'd probably let his supplies dwindle. "Pretty slim pickings in here. Come on. We're going to the café and you can buy me a piece of pie."

"Pie? I don't want pie."

"You—" she pointed at him "—will be eating one of the daily specials. No argument. Mom always says a man with an empty stomach can't think. Or was that my sister, Anna?"

She ushered him out the door and hurried down the steps beside him. They crossed the town square and walked into the Pleasant Prairie Café. Only one table in the middle of the room was vacant. They sank into two of its chairs and picked up daily paper menus. Lucie looked behind the counter to the glass pie display and made her choice. She tapped his paper menu. "What looks good?"

He grimaced. "I just don't have much of an appetite."

"Too bad. You're eating and that's that."

The gray-haired, comfortably padded waitress stopped and delivered glasses of water. "Hi, there, Pastor. What can we do for you tonight?"

"Hi, Joan," Tanner said, perusing the menu.

Joan eyed Lucie. "You're Nate's cousin-in-law, right?"

Lucie thought over this designation. "Yeah, that's right."

"Well, we're just so glad you could come and help Sophie and Nate out."

"It was my pleasure. I've enjoyed my summer here." Lucie's chest tightened for a moment. She realized Pleasant Prairie had found a spot in her heart. Leaving it wouldn't be easy. Did Tanner's kiss have anything to do with that?

"I've seen you over at the park on Thursday evenings with those kids. That's been wonderful and you didn't even charge the parents or town nothing. That's real Christian of you."

"It's been fun." Lucie blushed at the woman's praise. "I was here to help with the boys anyway."

The waitress nodded and took Lucie's order for a

cup of coffee and blueberry pie à la mode. "Are you ready to order, Pastor, or do you need more time?"

"Bring me a cup of coffee, Joan, and I'll be ready when you come back," he promised.

"Well, if you want the fried chicken, you better put your order in now. It's just about gone."

Tanner paused.

"Go ahead, Joan," Lucie said. "Put an order in for the chicken. He had roast beef last night at Sophie's table."

Tanner opened his mouth, closed it and then nodded. "She's right."

Joan chuckled and walked away. "I've heard about you two."

"What did she mean by that?" Tanner's brow crinkled.

Lucie smiled at him. "We've had enough *conflicts of opinion* across the street in that park—in front of God and everyone—that I'm sure a few stories have made the rounds about us." For some reason, Joan's comment hadn't bothered her. She'd been honored to hear her name and Tanner's connected. They'd argued, but they'd done some good together.

"Oh." He didn't look pleased.

Amused, Lucie watched Joan put in the order and swing behind the counter to snag cups for their coffee and the pot.

"I guess you two have heard about the layoff at the packing plant," Joan said as she poured two cups of coffee for them.

Lucie nodded.

"It seems a real shame. We were just getting to know some of the new people and now they'll all be leaving. Do you want your pie now or when I serve the preacher?"

"When you serve him," Lucie replied.

A retired farmer in overalls and a feed cap, sitting next to them, leaned over. "I think the town council ought to do something about it. I think I'll go on Wednesday evening and ask them what they intend to do about this."

"What do you mean, Henry?" Joan asked. "They can't keep the plant open."

"I know, but something should be done." The wrinkles on the man's leathery face pulled together as he stressed his point. "The new people are here and we should try to keep them here. If this town keeps shrinking, pretty soon there won't be any town here."

"That's right." Henry's companion joined in, his yellow-and-green feed cap bill bobbing in agreement. "If those new people hadn't come, JC over at the grocery would have had to shut down last year. Least, that's what he told me."

"Oh, dear," Joan worried aloud, "I wouldn't want us to lose the grocery. I don't want to have to drive all the way to Ames to buy groceries."

"Well, when those people out at the Shangri-La leave, that's what's going to happen," Henry said. Then both he and his companion rose to pay their bills.

Lucie considered Henry's comments.

One by one, the other diners finished eating, paid and left. The little café quieted. Joan delivered the fried chicken and the pie to their table and left them alone while she sat in the back to take her break. Tanner said a brief, quiet grace and picked up his fork.

"Well?" Lucie propped her hands under her chin. "What are we going to do about this?"

He stared at her. "What can *we* do? I can't afford to buy the factory and keep it open."

"I know you can't. What can we do to keep the newcomers here?"

He buttered his large homemade biscuit. "You don't understand. They need jobs to stay. And there aren't any jobs here."

"Well, I found that out myself. Replacing me as church secretary when I finally leave won't add much to the job pool here." Saying that she was leaving made her heart give a little jerk.

Tanner began eating his golden chicken, mashed potatoes and homemade gravy.

Lucie forked up a bite of juicy pie and vanilla ice cream. She let her mind go free, thinking, considering, letting ideas float in and out of her mind freely. Finally, she asked a question, "How far is Des Moines from here?"

"About twenty miles."

She took another bite and savored the creamy sweetness. "That's not far to drive for a job. Do some people live here and work in Des Moines?"

"A few, but we can't compete with the more fashionable subdivision communities closer to Des Moines that are bedroom communities.''

She didn't think Maria could afford to live in one of those, anyway. Why was he bringing that up? ''What about Ames?''

''About a fifteen-minute drive.''

Lucie felt a smile curve her lips. ''That sounds promising.''

Tanner eyed her. ''Where is this going?''

She leaned forward about to speak and then she paused. It was time to get him to contribute ideas. *I can't hold your hand forever, Tanner. I won't be here forever.* That tight feeling squeezed her heart again. ''You tell me, *padre,*'' she asked with bravado.

Tanner's face was a sight to behold. As he chewed, he screwed his face up as though he was in pain. Finally, he said, ''Do you mean the folks at Shangri-La might stay here and commute to Des Moines or Ames?''

She nodded. ''Why not?''

He stirred his fork in his mashed potatoes. ''Because most of them have older vehicles that aren't reliable in the winter.''

''Okay, and?''

''Most of them work for around twice the minimum wage. That's enough to make it cost-effective to drive to the packing plant outside of town and live at the trailer court here. Gas is high. If they decide to stay in Iowa, it would be more cost-effective for them to move to Des Moines, where there is public transportation and jobs.''

She scooped up another purpley blueberry-ice cream bite, letting it melt on her tongue. "Good points, every one of them. Now how can we turn those around so that the newcomers and the other people around here who still worked at the packing plant can stay in Pleasant Prairie?"

"What?"

She gave him an exaggerated sigh. "Bond, think out of the box for once. We want to keep people *here,* so how do we do it? You and I need a brainstorming session and come up with some ideas."

"But…what…can…we…do…with…just ideas?" he asked, venting his frustration with each word.

She punched his biceps. "You heard Henry. There's a town council meeting in two days."

"And you expect us—in just two days—to come up with ideas, a plan that the town council will act on?"

"Of course I do. Now finish that supper and we've got a lot of thinking and talking to do—"

"That's not enough time! We need time to pray—"

"Didn't we already have this discussion?" She put her hands on her hips, daring him. "These layoffs didn't take God by surprise. We'll pray and let God lead us."

"In just two days?" His eyebrows nearly lifted to his hairline.

She grinned at him and took a big bite of pie and ice cream. "That's the plan, man."

Chapter Thirteen

Two days had passed since Lucie had convinced Tanner to try to persuade the town council to take action. The town hall wasn't in the county courthouse where Lucie had mistakenly thought it would be. It was a small white frame building, only one room large over a basement and it stood alone on the east road out of town. Tanner drove the two of them up to join the other cars parked on the gravel lot that hugged the little building on three sides. Just beyond the parking lot, cornfields rustled in the breeze. Early crickets chanted, tuning up for the fall chorus, and a brown locust hopped around Lucie's feet as Tanner opened the car door for her.

When she stood, she paused to smooth her skirt and then she looked up at Tanner. Was he up for this? His face was drawn, dark circles ringed the transparent skin beneath his brown eyes. "You look like you haven't slept," she grumbled, and with a proprietary manner, smoothed the crisp cloth of his dark suit jacket.

"With a two-day deadline, I didn't have much time to prepare," he grumbled back at her.

"I'm not responsible for the timing," she said brightly, trying to edge him out of his gloom. "Now, this is important to a lot of people. We'll get further with smiles."

"Smile?" He looked as if he'd forgotten what the word meant, much less how to do it.

"Yes, a smile of confidence, supreme confidence. We've come to share ideas. We're a team with God, remember?"

He exhaled a long-suffering gust of oxygen and looked ready to argue the point with her.

"Part of succeeding is looking like you believe you will," she cut in before he could launch his latest lecture.

His crimped up his mouth and scowled at her.

She rose on her toes and kissed his crimped mouth.

A look of shock covered his face and then he leaned forward, kissing her in return.

She giggled against his lips, trying to ignore the warm current rippling through her veins. Breaking their connection, she stepped back and looked up. Tanner was smiling at her.

She gave him a cat-in-the-cream grin in return and thought, *Later, Tanner.* Her thought startled her. *What am I doing kissing Tanner?*

Pushing this thought from her mind, she smoothed her hands down his jacket sleeves. "Now that's what I wanted to see."

"Way to go, Preacher!" a voice came from behind them.

Lucie and Tanner turned as one to observe Henry, the farmer from the café, give Tanner a thumbs-up.

"Sorry," Tanner mumbled, and closed the car door.

"Hey!" Henry crowed, "I just wish I had a pretty young thing kissing me in the parking lot. Didn't know you had it in you."

Lucie waved at Henry while Tanner gave the retired farmer a stiff, but friendly nod. Then she felt Tanner put his hand low against her spine and usher her across the gravel and up the four steps. His touch made her breathless.

Inside, the town hall smelled musty and felt stuffy. She let her gaze rove over the scene. Around the narrow room, men were at the old frame windows grunting as they tried to force them open—with limited success. Another two men were plugging in oscillating pole fans to circulate the air and another was propping open the doors at each end of the building for a cross breeze.

"Mosquitoes will be attending the meeting with us tonight," she muttered to Tanner. Of course, he tried to sit in the rear, but she strode ahead and parked herself on an antique folding chair in the middle of the room. She smoothed her sleeveless cotton dress again and read the ancient black chalkboard at the front of the room on which an agenda had been scribbled in white. "Someone needs to have a few lessons in penmanship," she murmured to Tanner as he muttered to himself beside her.

"Huh?"

She nudged him in the ribs. "Lighten up. You'll be great."

"I wish you'd stop poking and punching me," he grumbled into her ear.

His warm breath tickled her ear and she rubbed it. Leaning close she whispered into his ear, "I'll be happy to if you stop needing to be nudged. We're here, and get that confident smile back on your face...or I'm kissing you again. You have five seconds. Now hit it!"

She glanced up at him and he suddenly smiled.

She chortled quietly to herself. *Okay, Lord, I got him here and have him smiling. The rest is up to You. Please bless his words with the power of persuasion and enter the hearts here and fill them with attention and sympathy. We need You.*

After the council was satisfied that they had enough air circulating, the meeting was gaveled to order. Lucie studied the five board members—the chairman in the middle, a gruff-sounding man in blue jeans with his shirtsleeves rolled up.

To his right, a man with a bushy mustache. Next was a man with thinning gray hair and a sour expression, and at the end was a thin man who had sharp eyes, his glance flitting restlessly around the room. On the chair's right sat a wizened man in neatly pressed but worn overalls who looked like he had to have been over ninety. Leave it to Pleasant Prairie to have a nonagenarian on the town council!

On the scribbled agenda, "New Business" was, of course, listed last. Lucie settled back against the uncomfortable chair and looked over the people—mostly blue-jeaned farmers and some of their wives in dark cotton slacks and pastel blouses—around her. But the presence of the man beside her claimed most of her attention.

From the corner of her eye, she studied the clean line of his hair clipped neatly around his ear. Thanks to their days at the ball diamond, his neck glowed with a healthy tan. She liked the way his jaw was set so firm and determined. Tanner might be hard to get started, but when he took on a challenge, he put everything into it.

Minutes crept by, agenda point by agenda point.

Tanner tried to concentrate on the boring discussions of matters of no interest to him. Lucie, sitting so close beside him, monopolized his attention. In the drab room, occupied with mostly farmers in denim, she stood out in her tropical print dress—all turquoise, pinks, and yellow—like an exotic bird trooping with crows.

He admitted to himself that if it hadn't been for her nudging, he wouldn't be here tonight. And he realized that she was right; he had to be here tonight, not at next month's meeting. A month from now would have been too late. People from Shangri-La and others in Pleasant Prairie would already have put For Sale or For Rent signs on their houses and be packing to leave with no one to take their places. No one could hang around without a job for long. A month's unemployment was too long for most.

Lucie shifted in her seat.

Tanner had been thinking about her a lot. She was a special lady. She'd spent the summer taking care of her cousin's family. She'd scrimped along on the few dollars a week the church had paid her to help him with clerical jobs. She'd forgone looking for a full-time job for the fall and the school year would start in barely two weeks. Pleasant Prairie wasn't even her home, but she cared about what happened to it. Her presence here tonight proved that. He was warmed straight through just thinking of her selfless giving. Did Pleasant Prairie understand how lucky they'd been to have Lucie Hansen here this summer?

I'm lucky, too.

Before he could pursue this thought, finally he heard the words he'd been waiting for, "Is there any new business to be discussed tonight?"

Lucie nudged Tanner. "Good luck."

He rose. "I have something to discuss."

"Okay, Pastor," the chairman intoned, "go ahead."

Tanner stepped into the aisle. "I'm sure you're all aware that the packing plant has been sold."

Murmurs rustled through the crowd. "That's what

I come to talk about," Henry spoke up. "Something's got to be done."

This support heartened Tanner.

The chairman frowned at Henry. "Let's follow proper order. The preacher has the floor."

"Over the past few days, I've compiled some statistics," Tanner continued, looking down at his notes. "Looking up census records. Starting in 1960, Pleasant Prairie's population was 11,652. In 1970, it was 9,678. The eighties, because of the severe farm recession, the population sank to 4,871."

"This is ancient history—" the member with the bushy mustache interrupted.

The crowd spoke up before Tanner could reply. "Let him talk!" "Shut up!" "This is important." "Go on, Preacher! Tell them!"

"Go get 'em." Lucie said the words just loudly enough for him to hear.

Tamping down his pleasure at this rally of support, Tanner cleared his throat. "By 1990, the population declined to 3,534. Finally, in 2000, we were down to the present number, 2,890."

He looked to the board, praying for them to take his words seriously. "These numbers are reflected in the ever-declining attendance numbers at my church over the same years. I might add that in those forty years, Pleasant Prairie lost three churches that had been here for over a century. The schools lost students, making it necessary to close the local high school and merge with Dailey."

He'd prayed without ceasing every waking moment for two solid days for God's power at this moment and suddenly he felt it. "I contacted the principal at the grade school and he says if they lose another fifty students, he will have to lay off two teachers. Any more and our school will close and Pleasant Prairie elementary students will have to be bused to Dailey, also."

"We already know all that," the chairman said. "What's your point?"

Tanner felt enthusiasm, power coursing within. "My point is obvious. The packing plant is the last remaining industry in this town. The agricultural community alone doesn't have the numbers to support the schools or businesses in town. If Pleasant Prairie doesn't do something to keep the people who will be unemployed this fall, it will again lose population. It will lose tax revenue. It will lose voting clout. We may be a ghost town by the census in 2010."

"What do you expect us to do about it?" the board member with the thinning hair demanded. "We can't keep the plant open."

"Something's got to be done!" Henry called out. Others clamored with similar sentiments.

With a smile and an outstretched arm, Tanner turned to Lucie. "Gentleman, I give you the idea person." Tanner's tone and smile spoke of pride in her.

Glowing with his affirmation, she popped up and stepped into the aisle beside him. "Chair and board members, I'm Lucie Hansen—"

"We know who you are," the bushy mustache barked. "You're not even a resident here—"

"Let her talk!" The gathering exploded. One man called out, "At least, she's prettier to look at than you five!"

The uneasy board members looked at each other and then subsided.

Lucie beamed at them. "Gentlemen, as I told Tanner the other day, we have to think outside the box. Now, Pleasant Prairie has an ace up its sleeve that it hasn't played...until now."

"And what's that, miss?" the chair asked. The board members watched her intently.

Lucie gave them a smile crafted to charm. "Pleasant Prairie is within easy driving distance to two cities that can use the workers..."

The thinning hair member tried to interrupt her again and the bushy mustache joined in.

Tanner grunted with antagonism and took a step forward.

She raised her hand. "Uh. Uh. Uh." She shushed them. "Let me finish, please." She stared at them until they clamped their mouths shut. "Now Tanner has just said that you will be losing tax revenue and sending kids to other schools by bus. Wouldn't it make more sense to rent a bus to pick up local residents here and bus them to the job centers, employment agencies in Ames and Des Moines daily and then bus them home each evening—keeping them living and shopping in Pleasant Prairie—"

"But they'll leave when they get jobs outside of t—'' bushy mustache horned in.

"No," Lucie cut him off, "they won't—*if* the same bus takes them to these new jobs in Des Moines and Ames. I mean, to the public transportation centers in those cities, and then picks them up in the same place each evening." A thoughtful silence greeted this.

"People don't like to move if they don't have to," Lucie continued, "so what Pleasant Prairie needs to do is make it easy for them to stay put. Something as simple as bus transportation could make all the difference."

"But that bus would only benefit part of the population," the bushy mustache growled. "That's not fair."

"Why wouldn't it be fair," Lucie said with a persuasive smile, "if everyone is allowed to ride the bus for the same small fee? Some residents might only use it once a week or once a month to spend a day in one of those cities. But it would be available to anyone." She lifted her hands in a gesture that said How can you argue with that?

"Nobody would have a problem with that kind of bus," Henry said, standing. "In fact, I never get to Des Moines because I don't want to bother with driving in that traffic. I'd use that bus once a month and I know my wife would use it more. She's always getting a bunch of ladies together and driving to Ames for lunch and shopping."

Lucie gave Henry a grateful smile. Tanner rose and drew near her.

For the first time, the nonagenarian board member heaved himself to his feet and introduced himself to Lucie as Milton Grosinger. "There's another thing we haven't discussed." He looked to his fellow board members, gaining their full attention. "I didn't like that scene that took place on the Fourth of July. A lot of people didn't. That mother said her son had been accused of snatching that purse because he was Mexican-American."

Lucie blinked. She couldn't have said it better herself.

Bushy mustache tried to interrupt; the nonagenarian forestalled him with an upraised hand. "I don't want people saying we didn't try to keep the newcomers because some of them still speak Spanish or their skin's a few shades darker. This pastor here—" he nodded toward Tanner "—has been helping the newcomers feel more at home here. I like that.

"Our town has always welcomed strangers from the very beginning. I can almost remember that myself." Milton grinned. "Maybe this bus idea won't pan out, but we gotta show that we're trying to keep the people we've got and maybe that will bring more people." His speech finished, he sat down.

Lucie was impressed by the total silence that followed. Obviously, his words had had an effect. What would happen now? Tanner took her hand.

The board members looked at each other. The chair cleared his throat. "Will someone make a motion?"

The member with the observant eyes, who hadn't spoken, raised his hand. "I make a motion that I, acting for the board, rent a bus or two and hire drivers to take people to Ames and Des Moines and advertise this and take reservations."

Lucie held her breath.

"There's too many points—" the bushy mustache growled.

"Is there a second to that motion?" the chair ignored him.

"I second it," the thinning hair said.

"All in favor, say aye," the chair continued.

Three board members said, "Aye."

Lucie reached for Tanner's other hand and squeezed both.

"All against say nay."

"Nay!" the bushy mustache shouted.

"The motion passes with a simple majority." The chair banged his gavel. "Meeting adjourned."

With a whoop, Lucie leaped into the air like a cheerleader. *Thank you, Lord!*

Tanner grabbed her around the waist and lifted her off her feet. "We did it! Praise God!" He planted a kiss square on her mouth and wrapped his arms around her, his heart pounding with victory and from holding Lucie close.

Later, Tanner sat on a dark green park bench, with Lucie in the crook of his arm, not wanting the evening to end. Night had fallen. The streetlights glowed, lighting the town square. A cooler breeze had blown up, dissipating the heavy heat of the day and whisking away mosquitoes.

Flushed with victory, he and Lucie had spent nearly an hour chatting with the board members and other citizens who'd attended the meeting. Except for the one who'd voted nay, everyone had wanted to talk. Hope for the future had shone on their faces and glowed inside Tanner still.

Finally, he'd driven Lucie back into town and invited her to enjoy a few moments of peace on the town square with him.

The church bells sounded. Out of habit, he lifted his wrist and checked the time. It was indeed after ten.

"I should take you home," he said, taking in the floral scent from her hair.

Lucie giggled. "That's the third time you've said that. I'll let you know when I'm ready to drive myself home. I brought the Bomb to the parsonage, remember?"

Tanner hadn't forgotten, but somehow that knowledge hadn't meant anything. It seemed he had entered the town hall his usual self tonight and came out a different man. He knew that time was ticking away as usual, but that mattered somewhere else. He couldn't be parted from Lucie. Not tonight. Not this special night.

His arm gathered her warmth and softness closer.

He didn't remember laying his arm around her shoulders, but he couldn't imagine his arm anywhere else. "You're wonderful, Lucie."

She beamed at him, smoothing his cheek with her hand. "You were great tonight. Where did you get those statistics?"

"Off the Internet, at the Census Bureau's Web site. I had even more in case I needed them."

"More? What kind?" Her eyes widened.

"Property tax revenues from different decades. School enrollment figures."

"Wow! You were loaded for bear." She ran her fingers through the hair over his forehead.

The sensation this brought made his whole body tighten. "Well, you said you'd take care of the ideas and I volunteered to impress the board with facts to convince them to go with your idea."

She turned and pressed closer to him. "We do make a great team."

He reveled in her softness. Unable to stop himself, he tucked her closer. A great team. She was right. They'd been a team since that first trip to Shangri-La. When he looked back over the summer, he felt a sense of accomplishment.

The ball games in the mornings, the evening games, the Bible study, the promise of more Bible studies. Just small steps, but they'd added up to progress, progress he wouldn't have made if it had been left up to him. He would never forget this moment.

"How are you doing about getting people lined up

to work Nate's harvest?'' She looked up at him, her eyes at the level of his chin.

He gazed down into her huge blue eyes, so clear, so honest. He bent down and kissed her pert nose. ''What?''

Lucie laughed and pulled away slightly. Tanner's nearness was intoxicating. ''Pay attention. Who have you got signed up to work Nate's harvest?''

''Mort and three other neighbors.''

''Will that be enough?'' she asked.

He slid his forefinger around her ear, tucking a tawny curl behind it. ''I'd like to have it all done in one or two days. The ones I just mentioned said they'd spread the word. Usually, all the neighboring farmers will pick one day in the fall and all show up with their combines and grain trucks work until the crop is in.''

''Great.'' Lucie sighed, leaning her head back on his arm. ''Then all our problems are solved.'' She ticked them off on her fingers one by one. ''Nate's home and getting better all the time. Zoë's back to being herself, under a doctor's care for the baby and in good hands with my mother and Sophie. The Mexican-Americans are becoming a part of Pleasant Prairie…. Did you hear the senior board member? I wanted to kiss him.''

''You did kiss him,'' he teased, luxuriating in her relaxed pose, somehow so intimate.

She whooped with laughter and then went on with her recital. ''And now we've got something started that may keep most of the newcomers and some other residents in town. Wow. Do I feel good or what?''

''Lucie, I couldn't have done it without you.'' This admission filled him with joy and another feeling....

Tanner's words sizzled through Lucie, igniting joy and deepening her attraction to him. ''Oh, of course, you could. You just needed a nudge.'' Playfully, she poked his ribs with her elbow, trying to lighten the mood.

He caught her hand and held it. ''Your little nudges may have irritated me at first, but I like what happens when you give me a push. I don't know why I can't get things off the ground on my own.''

His hand held hers so tenderly, as if she were as fragile as a dragonfly's wing. Her heart raced. ''You just don't want to make a mistake. That's all.'' Tanner's words were giving her hope. Her emotions soared—joy, hope, attraction. Maybe she'd been wrong about what being married to a clergyman would be like. Certainly, Tanner would never rain on her parade.

He inhaled. ''You may be right. Doesn't making a mistake ever bother you?''

Would it really be a mistake to fall in love with you? She shrugged. ''I just get carried away. Sometimes I may jump in and find myself over my head, but then I just start swimming for shore. And sometimes I plunge in and only get wet for my efforts. But I always think it's better to try something than to just sit there and maybe miss a perfect opportunity.''

Tanner lifted her hand and caressed it with his lips. "I think you're wonderful. Lucie, don't leave Pleasant Prairie. Stay here."

His tender kiss sent a warm glow coursing through her. Lucie gazed up into his eyes and, reading their invitation, leaned forward.

He bent and kissed her again.

The touch of his lips sent shards of excitement through her. Her heart sang with joy while her head was full of questions. *Am I in love? Is Tanner the one, my one and only?*

Tanner tucked her nearer and murmured in her ear, "Tell me you'll stay, Lucie. I—"

A car screeched to a halt in front of them.

Lucie looked away from Tanner.

A woman got out and slammed the door. "Tanner, darling, is that you?"

Tanner stiffened and freed Lucie abruptly. "Mother? What are you doing here?"

Chapter Fourteen

A week later, at Sophie's front door—Vita, Tanner's mother, made another of her dramatic entrances, calling out, "I'm here. Vita's here!"

Lucie suppressed a giggle. Vita's flamboyance tickled her.

Dorothy called from the stove where she was bringing water to boil. "We're in the kitchen, Vita!"

Vita swirled in, wearing a designer aqua silk pant suit—to can tomatoes at Sophie's. Lucie looked at Sophie, who looked back at her and rolled her eyes. Vita arranged herself on the nearest kitchen chair.

Tanner's mother had a "distinctive style," according to Dorothy. Vita had cut quite a noticeable swath through Pleasant Prairie. During the first week of Vita's visit, when Lucie went to town, people stopped her to ask who "that woman was." No one believed her when she told them Vita was Tanner's mother.

Dorothy turned from the stove and smiled. "That's such a pretty outfit, Vita. And cool, too. But you'll need this to keep from ruining it." Dorothy lifted a full apron in a faded yellow-and-gray print off one of the hooks on the back of the kitchen door. She offered it to Vita.

"Oh?" Vita looked at it, her expression dubious. "My, how quaint." She forced a smile as she accepted the apron, gingerly donning it.

"I really appreciate you helping out." With backward glances, Sophie lifted Carly out of her high chair and washed the squirming baby's face and hands at the sink. "I have to drive Nate in for physical therapy again today and the tomatoes are ripening so fast, we need to get them put up for the winter."

Lucie knew the bushels of tomatoes had been weighing on her cousin's mind. Lucie couldn't figure out why this was a problem. She could think of dozens of ways to get rid of ripe tomatoes, none of which included work. And store brand tomatoes were cheap! Time and sweat definitely counted for more in Lucie's estimation! But Sophie wanted to keep the tomatoes, so canning had been inevitable.

Nate swung into the kitchen on his crutches with Tanner behind him. Lucie felt a thrill go through her and she winked at Tanner.

"Son!" Vita made a theatrical gesture toward the apron. "Look how domestic I am today!"

"Oh." Tanner looked as if he didn't know what to say and then his expression became skeptical. He sidled over to Lucie. "Are you sure you want to do this, Mother?"

Lucie had wondered that herself. But she'd been too glad to have help to look a gift horse in the mouth.

"Of course!" Vita exclaimed. "It will be an adventure! And everyone is pitching in to help this little family. I can't stand by watching while you've all volunteered so faithfully."

At this accolade, Tanner looked uncomfortable.

Coming to his rescue, Dorothy walked over and patted his shoulder. "Your mother will do fine and we'll take good care of her. Now, go on home and write that sermon. Come back for supper. Sophie will pick up a bucket of fried chicken and the works in Ames and bring it back with her. Unless you want to feast on freshly canned tomatoes?"

Tanner looked mollified and took Lucie's hand.

At his touch, she felt herself grinning.

"Okay, Dorothy, whatever you say," Tanner assented. "Mother, see you later." He paused at the doorway, letting Sophie and Nate go ahead of him. "Lucie, walk me to the car?"

With both mothers watching her, Lucie flushed pink. But wanting a moment alone with him, she accompanied Tanner. Outside, she waited while he saw that Nate got safely down the back steps and into the minivan.

Then as they walked to his gray sedan, she swung his hand back and forth and gave a little skip.

"I can't come up with one reason why *my* mother

thinks she's capable of canning tomatoes.'' Tanner leaned back against his car. ''She doesn't even cook!'' Tanner vented as he pulled Lucie to him.

Lucie resisted him at first and then gave in, putting her arms around his neck. ''Oh, give her some credit for at least volunteering.'' She chuckled. ''I'm glad your mother offered to help. If it didn't mean saddling my mother with the whole canning thing, I would have bailed out myself. I'm not the domestic type, either.''

''I just can't figure out what's going on with her,'' Tanner fretted. ''She's acting…odd…not like herself. I keep wondering…''

''Wondering?'' Lucie rubbed her nose against his in an Eskimo kiss, but he refused to lighten up.

''Wondering if her engagement is off. But her fiancé has called her several times and she says the wedding has been postponed—not canceled. I just don't get it.''

This was classic Tanner—worry-worry. ''She's only been here a week.'' Lucie stood on tiptoe and pulled his forehead down to meet hers. ''Just go with the flow,'' she said, nose to nose with him. ''Everything comes out in the wash, my mom always says.''

Finally focusing on her, Tanner's gaze met hers. He tightened his hold around her. ''I still can't believe that you and I haven't *even* been able to get time for a decent date. All we get to do is meet for coffee, ball practice—''

''Ah, yes, and suppers at Sophie's with my mother and yours watching our every move. So romantic,''

Lucie added with a grin. "You have to stop sweeping me off my feet."

He bent down and kissed her.

Lucie savored the moment and then pulled away. "Go on. You've got a sermon to write and I have bushels of tomatoes to scald. Hey! Wait! Now that I think about it, I'd rather write that sermon—"

"Not a chance." Tanner chuckled and hurried behind the steering wheel. "I'm looking forward to my few quiet hours in the church basement."

"Coward!" Lucie waved him off and stood, watching his car kick up dust down the gravel drive.

Over the past week, she and Tanner hadn't spoken about their feelings. They'd had few moments alone. But ever since the night of the town council meeting, they'd become a couple.

It was as if they'd made a connection that didn't need words. Time would tell if this were love, true love, the kind her parents shared. *If I've fallen in love with a preacher, God must have a droll sense of humor.* Lucie sighed and turned and walked back to the steamy kitchen.

Dorothy stood beside Vita at the stove. "Lucie, I'm going to let Vita have the job of spooning the tomatoes just in and out of the hot bath to loosen their skins. You and I will sit at the table and peel and pack them into jars."

Lucie nodded and sat down. The table had a laundered vinyl tablecloth over it. Quart jars, fresh from the dishwasher, sat on one side of the table with a clean white cloth over them. Two shallow nine-by-thirteen pans and two paring knives waited for use.

"Here, Vita, see how the skin is crinkling?" Dorothy demonstrated. "Use this slotted spoon to dip and then lift the tomatoes out individually and put them on this platter. Tell us when it's full."

"Looks simple enough," Vita declared.

Lucie picked up the paring knife and a warm tomato her mother had scalded and began peeling off the skin. The three women worked as the window air conditioner buzzed, trying to keep them cool in spite of the two kettles of bubbling water: one for scalding the tomatoes and the other, the hot canning bath.

"This brings back memories," Vita said, her back to them. "I helped my grandmother and mother can tomatoes and make jellies when I was growing up."

"Really?" Dorothy commented. "Me, too."

"Me, three," Lucie teased.

"Yes." Vita went on as if she hadn't heard them, "My grandfather and father were both clergy and as poor as the proverbial church mice. Parishioners brought us produce and we preserved or did without."

Lucie's antenna picked up. From Vita's too-casual voice, she sensed that this was not casual conversation. This topic had a purpose for Vita. Lucie tensed.

"That's one of the reasons I was so opposed to Tanner going into the ministry. Of course, it's a wonderful way of giving of one's self. But it's such a financial sacrifice for the man *and* his family." Vita paused.

Lucie felt it was a pregnant pause, an uncomfortable one. What was the woman's point? Everyone knew no one went into the ministry for the big bucks.

"I could have warned him—" Vita gave a sorrowful, world-weary sigh "—that he'd have a hard time finding a woman willing to make those kinds of sacrifices."

"Oh, I don't know about that," Dorothy said in a gentle tone. "Tom has always provided for his family. And times have changed. Churches expect to pay professional salaries to pastors now or they don't keep them. Pastors don't take vows of poverty in this generation."

Way to go, Mom! Lucie silently cheered.

"Well, I wish Tanner's fiancée had seen it that way. I told Tanner how it would be. When he let her know he was going to seminary, she gave him back his ring."

Lucie absorbed this bombshell without giving any visible sign. So Tanner had been hurt. *Poor Tanner.*

"It's probably for the best, then," Dorothy said, packing tomatoes into another quart. "If she wasn't called to be a minister's wife, it wasn't meant to be."

Am I meant to be a minister's wife? Lucie peeled another warm tomato. *How did a person know that?*

Mikey and Danny burst through the back door. "Lucie! Lucie! We're hot! Can we turn on the sprinkler?"

Happy for the distraction, Lucie rose and wiped off

her hands. "Sure. I'll come and make sure you get it situated right."

"Can Fella run through it, too?" Danny asked.

"Now that he's all healed up, sure." Lucie walked to the door. The boys ran back outside and she turned to Vita and paused. She didn't want to let Vita's meddling go unanswered.

Lucie drew upon her reserves. What did it matter that Tanner had a broken engagement, except that she felt bad that he'd been hurt? She gave Vita a mischievous look. "Well, you know, some engagements are made to be broken. I've broken one or two myself," she joked, and closed the door behind her.

The thought that Vita might be less than thrilled that her son was "involved" with Lucie dragged at her painfully, but she brushed it aside. After all, Vita had only known her one week. And besides, she and Tanner were a long way from getting engaged. *We're not even dating yet!*

Another few weeks had zipped by. School would be starting on Monday. With dusk tinting the sky, Lucie watched as the final Thursday-evening ball game neared its end. Tonight's game was special because many parents had joined in playing on their kids' teams. That had put Lucie out of a job as pitcher. Tanner hovered near his team on the batting bench. In white shorts and a blue shirt, he looked too handsome for her peace of mind. Days in the sun had only done him good.

Sidelined, Lucie felt oddly lonely, so to be near Sophie and Nate, she sat in the lowest bleacher. Vita and Dorothy sat behind them.

Vita was still visiting her son and had made not one move to tell him why she was in town or when she planned to leave.

Lucie tried to like her, but couldn't warm to her for several reasons. She felt that Vita didn't like her, didn't want her near her son and was keeping something from her son. Lucie tried not to take the rejection personally, but she was used to being liked. It hurt. *You're going to have to help me out here, Lord.*

Sarah Louise Kremer hit the ball and Miguel ran for home. He made it and the stands went wild. He bounded up to Lucie and she gave him a congratulatory hug. "Way to go!"

Instead of going back to his team bench, he stayed beside Lucie and together they cheered his team to victory.

The mothers of the ballplayers had set a table of refreshments in the park's pavilion and everyone moved toward it. The evening ball games had succeeded in bringing the newcomers a step into the community. All around her, parents—homegrown and imported—chatted and nibbled cookies. Miguel hopped and skipped beside her. "Are you looking forward to school?" Lucie asked him.

"Yeah, I guess," the boy replied. "My mom is trying to find a job in Ames. She's got a interview tomorrow."

The town bus had been taking people to Des Moines and Ames every day for the past two weeks. Lucie felt a burst of satisfaction. God had blessed the seed she and Tanner had planted that night at the town hall. *We did something right, Lord! Thanks!* "Great. I hope she gets a job."

"Me, too. I don't want to move. I like snow, and my school here. We all get computer time every day and everything. My mom wants me to learn how to use them so I can get a good job when I grow up." At the refreshments table, Miguel filled both hands with cookies.

"Sounds like a plan," Lucie agreed, watching Tanner across the crowded pavilion. He was talking to a group of farmers, probably finalizing the plans for tomorrow's community harvest of Nate's crops. He'd organized this without even a push from her. Pride in Tanner blossomed in Lucie. He was such a good man.

"And I wanna be here when you and the *padre* get married," Miguel finished, and then rushed off to a friend who was waving at him.

Lucie shook her head ruefully. Everyone in Pleasant Prairie had her and Tanner married and in the parsonage and they hadn't had their first *real* date yet!

Turning, she found Vita facing her. Vita's expression did not reassure Lucie. Frankly, Vita's hovering was getting on Lucie's nerves.

"Hi! I'm going to get some lemonade. Want some?"

Vita shook her head.

"Oh, okay—"

"Lucie," Vita said with a sorrowful expression, "I think it's time I spoke up. I think you're a wonderful girl, so vibrant and lovely, but you just aren't the right woman for my son."

Lucie felt her anger spark. *That's it!* "Vita—"

"Now look at Dorothy. Your mother's the perfect pastor's wife—so reserved, yet friendly, so accommodating and…unassuming. But you're not like your mother, Lucie dear. You are cut from too colorful a cloth to make a preacher's wife. Your outspoken ways would empty out Tanner's church after the first week!" Vita smiled and patted Lucie's shoulder consolingly. "As the pastor's wife, you'd be a disaster! You must give up Tanner. It's what's best for him."

Lucie bit back a heated retort like "What business is it of yours?" Miguel's comment had only ruffled Lucie's feathers a touch. He was a kid, after all. But Vita should know better! And her words—"Your mother's the perfect pastor's wife"—hit Lucie squarely in the pit of her stomach. Fuming and afraid of what she might say, Lucie swung away and hustled to the other side of the pavilion.

Grinning from ear to ear, Tanner approached her with a glass of lemonade. "Thirsty?"

She eyed him, her lips pursed. Why couldn't he find time to take her out? Was Vita talking to him behind Lucie's back? And had he told his mother he planned to marry Lucie—without saying a word to her? "No," she snapped finally.

His eyes widened, but he merely held the plastic glass. "Hey, you'll be proud of me. I just got an idea and ran with it."

"Oh?" Vita's hurtful words played in her mind. *"You're a wonderful girl... You're not like your mother."*

"I'm going to start a computer class for adults in the church basement next week. And I'll need you, your talent at Spanish and your laptop Thursday evening."

He just takes it for granted that I'll stay here! Can't even make time to ask me out! Without a word to me, tells his mother... Lucie felt mad and sad at the same time, hot tears bubbled up in her eyes. "Sorry. I won't be here next week. I'm going home with my mom."

Hurt and her own fears ganged up on her. "And the next time you decide to discuss marrying me with your mother, you might let me in on it first!" Tears starting, she turned and ran to the Bomb. She squealed out of the parking lot.

The clouds in the sky the next morning were high cirrus, wispy veils of white. Lucie looked out the kitchen window to the gathering of farmers who would try to harvest Nate's crop in one day. On crutches, Nate stood among his neighbors, shaking hands. Sam Torres stood at his side. But Lucie's attention focused on Tanner.

A sour taste still lingered in her mouth from last night. She acknowledged that she had been rude to

Tanner, but she couldn't make herself venture outside to apologize. What could she say to him?

Why did Vita have to open her mouth and stir everything up? Why couldn't she have just let Lucie enjoy being with Tanner? Why had she forced Lucie to face the fact that she might not be the wife Tanner needed?

As Lucie worried her lower lip, the farmers took off in grain trucks and combines. Sam would drive Nate's grain truck with Nate along for the ride. Though Nate would have to rest at home after lunch, Lucie could see how happy he was to be able to at least be out in the harvest. Tanner and Ignacio got into another grain truck and followed Mort Hazelton in his combine out of the yard.

This was Tanner's first time helping. The combine would harvest and spew the grain into the truck until it was full and then Tanner and Ignacio would drive the load into town and empty it into the twin towering grain elevators there just like all the other teams.

This would be repeated by many combine-and-truck teams all day, until Nate's crop was harvested. And to save Sophie from cooking for the harvesters, an army of farmers' wives would be bringing covered dishes and vats of iced tea to be eaten at Sophie and Nate's. Lucie wasn't needed in the harvest or the feast.

Feeling superfluous, she went up to her room and flopped down on her bed. The worn cotton quilt felt soft against her cheek. She yawned. She hadn't slept much the night before.

What was she going to do now? Mikey and Danny would be in school next week. Nate was steady on his crutches and improving daily. Little Carly was trying to walk. The daily ball games in the park had ended. The school year that she'd hoped to have a teaching job for was starting and she was unemployed and broke. *Where do I go from here, Lord?*

A noise.

Lucie jerked up from her bed and rubbed her eyes. She must have dozed off.

The noise came again—the branches of the maple tree outside her window, stretching, scraping her window. Another gust and the green leaves shivered and bent lower. Lucie leaped up and hurried down the stairs. ''Sophie!''

The house was quiet. Lucie ran outside where the wind was kicking up dust. Zoë, Dorothy with Carly in her arms and Sophie stood in the yard, all looking skyward, even the baby. Fella came barking. Mikey and Danny ran from the barn toward their mother. Sophie clutched a battery-operated transistor radio in her hand. Static crackled from it.

''What's up?'' Lucie asked, also looking to the sky, now gray and roiling with ominous clouds.

''There was the threat of a storm today, but the weatherman said it would track north to Minnesota and miss us,'' Sophie said, her brow wrinkled.

''This just blew up out of nowhere,'' Dorothy said.

"That happens here," Sophie said. "Weather can change in an instant."

"What should we do?" Lucie raised her voice to be heard over the wind.

A grain truck roared up their lane and jerked to a stop beside them. Tanner jumped out. "We were on our way back from the elevator. You've heard the weather report?"

"The storm front's dropped south," Sophie nearly shouted, the wind intensifying.

"*¡Sí!*" Ignacio agreed, joining Tanner. "It looks bad."

"I don't trust that sky, and they're predicting dangerous winds." Tanner took his cell phone, a recent present from his mother, off his belt and flipped it open. "Sophie, use your CB and call to warn all the farmers just in case, though I'm pretty sure everyone is already getting their equipment out of the fields and heading for the nearest shelter."

"Is it a tornado?" Lucie asked.

Tanner shook his head. "They haven't said so, but we got a storm like this last summer and it wasn't a tornado—"

"It was a gustnado!" Sophie shouted as she ran for Nate's truck and his CB on the dash.

Tanner nodded, looking serious. "Straight line winds. The radar doesn't pick them up, but they can do the same damage as a tornado. I'm calling the verger. He lives right near St. Andrew's." Then he spoke into the phone, "Hey, this is Bond. Please go over to the church. Use the override and turn on the bells and keep them on. Open the basement doors in case people need to come there for shelter. Yeah, I'm afraid this storm is going to bring down trees.'' He snapped it shut.

"Why the bells?" Lucie asked. Everything was moving too fast. She didn't have time to think!

He gave her a grim look. "The town's warning siren is down. The bells will alert people in and near town that they should take shelter." He then called the parsonage and told his mother to go to the basement with no argument.

Lucie shivered, not just from alarm. A cool edge rushed in with the wind that was flapping her hair around her face and billowing her blouse.

Lightning crackled white overhead.

Thunder blasted, shaking the earth around Lucie's feet.

A torrent of rain poured down on them.

"Head for the cellar!" Sophie shrieked, running toward them.

Nate's vintage cellar's door opened to the yard. Fighting the wind, Lucie hurried her mother with the baby inside first. Tanner and Ignacio stood holding the wooden doors as a few pickups pulled into the yard— wives coming with dishes of food for lunch. They jumped out of their trucks and sprinted through the torrent to the cellar. The wind gusted nearly ripped one of the doors from Ignacio's hands.

Tanner and Ignacio pulled the doors inward and

then shoved the old wooden bar braced against the doors. The bar vibrated as the wind tried to rip the doors open.

Tanner came and folded Lucie into his arms. She shivered against his soaked shirt. She heard him murmuring prayers for the safety for them, for his mother at the parsonage and for their neighbors. The doors flapped and the wind whined and shrieked.

Images from TV news reports of trailer homes smashed and upended in high winds flashed in her mind. Pressing her face against his wet shirtfront, she prayed with him. *Lord, protect everyone but especially help those in the open fields and those in the trailer court! They don't have cellars! Anything could happen!*

Chapter Fifteen

Within minutes, the storm blew itself to the next county. Rain still fell, but the wind had lost its violence. While the rest of them hurried into Sophie's kitchen, Lucie jumped into Nate's truck. Tanner climbed behind the steering wheel. Both of them wanted the same thing—to find out if everyone had made it safely through the storm. "Do you know how to run this thing?" Tanner handed her the CB microphone from the dash as he drove out of the yard.

"I can fake it." She flipped the switch and the CB radio lights flared. She studied the mike and pushed in a button. "This is Lucie at Nate's farm. Anyone copy me?"

A voice crackled from the radio speaker. "This is Farmer One, back at you. Is the storm past?"

"Farmer One, it looks like it," Lucie responded. "The storm has moved east. Are you and your team okay?'' Her heart still pumped from a large dose of adrenaline.

''Back at you, Lucie. We made it back to my place before the winds hit. Have you heard from the other teams?''

''No, but the preacher and I are going to make the rounds, back at you.''

''Roger. We're heading in. Fields'll be too wet to harvest for several days. Out.'' Farmer One clicked off.

One by one, Lucie raised the others on the radio. ''That's a relief.''

He nodded. ''Thanks be to God.'' Tanner swiped his sleeve across the sweat on his forehead. ''We'll have to try again soon. Right now, I'm heading into town.''

Lucie noted Tanner's tension ease, but just a fraction. He still gripped the steering wheel and kept his jaw clamped as he drove. The roadside culverts rushed with rainwater. Mud smeared the road and branches littered it and the shoulder.

In town, they had to stop. A large maple had blown down, blocking Main Street near the park and church. Mitch from the nearby auto shop approached carrying a chain saw. He pulled its cord and the distinctive burring whine sounded. Tanner jumped out and went to help Mitch as he began cutting the trunk to clear the road.

Lucie got out to look around. She picked her way around the sopping-wet downed branches and leaves.

Suddenly a group of women and children, some from Shangri-La, found to her. Overjoyed, Lucie hugged Sammie Torres and then his mother. "You weren't at the trailer court?"

"We were but—" Mrs. Torres motioned to the white police cars parked nearby "—the police came through and picked up people and brought us to the church."

Miguel spoke up. "We were playing in the park and heard the bells ringing. A man there told us the *padre* wanted us to come into the basement, a bad storm was coming. I was scared!"

Lucie hugged him close, remembering her own fear in Sophie's dark storm cellar.

"Did you see my Sam?" Mrs. Torres asked.

Lucie nodded. "He's on his way back with Nate to the farm. They're both fine."

"*¡Gracias a Dios!*" Mrs. Torres pressed her hand to her heart.

"Yes, thank God," Lucie echoed.

"And I came over from the café," the waitress said, "and brought my customers, too. I'm so glad someone thought to ring the bells. It got me moving!"

Tanner returned to Lucie, gathering her close with an around her shoulders. "We've cleared a narrow lane. We can get through. I want to see if everyone's okay at Shangri-La."

Lucie stayed close to him, sensing his urgency.

"Most everyone was still at the plant," Mrs. Torres

said, "and a lot of the kids were here in the park. I
think the police got us all out of the trailer court."

"Good, but I want to see for myself," Tanner insisted, hurrying Lucie back to the truck.

Lucie prayed they'd not find anyone hurt. She'd
come to love the people in this town.

As they drove through the entrance to the trailer
court, they saw that several pine trees had been blown
down. Branches littered the streets and patches of
lawn. Two trailers on the western edge had been swept
off their cement block foundations. A police car was
already there and a policeman waved to them, calling,
"No one's here! They all got out!"

Lucie turned to Tanner and threw her arms around
him. "You were wonderful!" Her pride in his quick
action and leadership flowing out in tears and laughter.

Tanner crushed her deeper into his embrace. He
bent and kissed her.

Night had come. A cool breeze after the storm had
made Sophie turn off the air-conditioning and open
the windows. Everyone had gone to bed except for
Lucie and Tanner.

In a subdued mood, she walked beside him to the
back porch. His mother was at home waiting for him.
Lucie recalled their first real kiss on this same back
porch and the kiss they'd shared this morning at the
trailer court. That kiss had swept away all her hurt and
anger from the night before. But where did they go
from here?

Tanner hesitated on the top step. "Can we talk?"

"We'd better," she said with a confidence she didn't feel. She sank down on the step and propped her elbows on her knees, waiting to see what he'd have to say. *Lord, have I been mistaken in what I feel or in what I thought this man felt for me?*

"I realize we haven't known each other that long, but..."

Lucie grinned. This was authentic Tanner, true to form in his let's-not-rush-into-anything mode. She leaned her cheek on his shoulder. "Time is relative."

"You're just out of college. I want you to have time to live on your own—"

She chuckled and decided to use her let's-get-to-the-point attitude. "I've lived on my own since I was eighteen. Now, are you proposing or trying to get out of proposing?"

"Lucie..." He shook his head. "Lucie..." He gazed at her and then threw his hands high. "Oh, so much for the sensible approach." He hugged her close. "I'm in love with you, you vibrant, slightly crazy, completely adorable woman! Will you marry me?"

Laughing aloud, she hugged him back and then pulled away to look into his face. "I'm in love with you, you wonderful, slightly stick-in-the-mud, absolutely gorgeous man! I will marry you."

"Then why were you so upset with me last night?" He kissed her ear.

Reveling in the tingling down her neck this ignited,

Lucie sighed. "First, I'm sorry I snapped your head off. Your mother had just made it clear that in her opinion I'm not the right girl for you—"

"I wondered if my mother had upset you. Don't worry. I'll set her straight—"

"Wait. Your mom wasn't the problem." She leaned against him, drawing on his strength to speak the truth. "You know me. I'm a free spirit!"

"I know that."

She pulled away to watch him to make certain he understood. "Ever since I was in my teens, I've been at odds with my mom. I didn't like how people all took advantage of her. She was always there for everyone and always sweet and always said just the right thing, unlike me—"

"And your point is?" he asked archly.

Lucie considered her answer, because it was an important one. "I just thought I could never be like that, be like my mom, so I made a promise to myself that I'd never marry—"

"A preacher." Tanner chortled.

Wrinkling her nose, she punched his arm. "So you see, your mom really didn't upset me, she just touched my sore spot. It was a shock to hear my own fears coming out of *her* mouth."

Tanner corralled her in his arms again. "Lucie, you are just the right kind of wife for this preacher. I've accomplished more this summer than I have in the year before you arrived. I have good intentions, but I admit it—I have trouble getting things started. You make me get busy and move. I like that.''

''We're a good team.'' She grinned and kissed him, hope for their future flooding her. ''And I've realized that my mom's one kind of pastor's wife. I'll just be another kind!''

Tanner took her face in his both his hands. ''I love you, Lucie.''

''I love you,'' she echoed.

Later, feeling a joy he'd rarely felt, Tanner drove into his one-car garage behind the parsonage. *Lord, help me break the news in just the right way. I don't want to widen the gap between my mother and me. Help this bring us closer.* Then he walked into his kitchen. His mother sat at the table, holding a mug of one of her herb teas between her hands. ''Hi, Mom.''

''Hi, dear. I thought this would calm my nerves. What a day.'' She leaned her head against the steaming mug. ''I don't think the last earth tremor in Thousand Oaks upset me this much.''

Tanner sat down at the table and a realization hit him. Before he broke the news about his engagement to Lucie, he needed the truth about his mother's coming here. ''I think it's time you tell me why you came for this visit.''

His mother looked away. ''Just wanted to see you—''

He took one of her hands. ''Tell me the truth.''

She set the mug down. "We haven't gotten along for so many years...."

"Ever since I decided to go to seminary."

She faced him. "I just didn't want you to have to live like I did as a child. We were so poor, and as the preacher's daughter, I had to be the perfect little girl." She tightened her lips. "I couldn't breathe, Tanner! And here you were willingly going into that... repressive, drab lifestyle! I couldn't believe it! I couldn't face it!"

Trying to understand, Tanner squeezed her hand. "Mother, money's not a problem. I'm paid well for a first pastorate in a small church. Most important, I felt God's calling. I love my job and believe me, I can breathe." *Especially with Lucie at my side.* "But this still isn't the reason why you came. What's wrong? Aren't you and Barry going to marry after all?"

"Barry? You thought...? No, dear." Now her lips crimped tighter. She blinked away tears. "All right." She steadied herself. "I had a scare...a bad mammogram...an inconclusive biopsy."

"Cancer?" Tanner asked, gripping her hands and feeling his stomach sink.

Exhaling, she leaned back against her chair and stared at the tabletop. "I'm fine! I had a few more tests and another biopsy and no cancer." She pulled his hands and pressed them to her cheek. "But it made me want to see you. I'm so sorry, son, for pushing you away. I love you so much. I shouldn't have done that!"

He gathered her into his arms and let her shed a few tears of relief on his shoulder. He patted her and prayed that she'd understand his choices. "I'm sorry that you were treated so badly as a child. That shouldn't have happened. But I think it's time you also made peace with God over it. He loves you, Mother, more than I am able to, and He didn't want you treated like that."

She pulled away and wiped her eyes. "I think you're right. Facing cancer turned my life upside down. I've done a lot of thinking since. And I've enjoyed the services at your church. I've gained a new peace here."

"I'm glad." He took a deep breath and plunged on. "I just asked Lucie to marry me."

"Oh! Tanner!" she shrilled. "Are you sure?"

He grinned. "We're just unofficially engaged for now. We love each other, but we aren't going to rush to the altar."

His mother frowned.

He patted her arm. "Mom, Lucie is the right woman for me. If I'm wrong, I'll pray that God lets both of us know long before we marry. Don't worry. Over this summer I've discovered that Lucie is just the wife I need. And I love her."

"Very well, Tanner." His mother still looked hesitant. "I'll pray that you two both do what's right."

Tanner kissed her cheek. "I couldn't ask for more than your prayers."

Epilogue

Lucie and Tanner stood behind their towering white-and-pink-rosed wedding cake, posing for the photographer. Lucie felt like a medieval princess in shimmering satin with dozens of seed pearls over the bodice of her long white gown, and Tanner looked gorgeous in a black-and-white tux—in her opinion!

The fragrance of fresh-cut lilacs filled St. Andrew's basement in Pleasant Prairie. A heady scent. Members of the church and friends had decorated the reception room with lilacs from their own bushes. And here or there a late tulip—red or yellow—spiced up a bouquet of the lavender flowers.

"Now, sweetheart, I've been worried about this cake thing." Tanner whispered in Lucie's ear. "Please don't smear that cake on my face, okay?"

"Ah, but this is so tempting. A once-in-a-life opportunity!" Brandishing a small square of the sweet confection, she chuckled wickedly. Instead, she kissed him and then carefully popped the morsel of cake into his mouth.

He, too, picked up a small square of cake and poised it over Lucie's mouth. ''Should I or shouldn't I?'' he taunted.

The gathering of guests laughed and encouraged him to have fun. Finally, he slipped the bite of cake into Lucie's mouth and then sealed it with a kiss.

Lucie savored the sweet frosting and the touch of her husband's lips as she gazed out at the basement full of friends. Pleasant Prairie had weathered the layoffs and the population had stayed. In fact, the town was growing as more newcomers came to live in the ''community that cares.''

Zoë had given birth to a beautiful little girl. Holding her tiny daughter, she stood between Lucie's mom and dad. Lucie's sister Anna and her husband had come with a baby, too. Lucie's first nephew was already six months old. Another blessing, Nate had left his crutches far behind and had his arm around Sophie. Carly chased her brothers around the fringe of the gathering. Even Fella and Sancho had been included.

Sam Torres had moved into a trailer on Nate's farm, where he worked now. Leaving the packing plant behind had been good for Sam. He even smiled once in a while. And this made it possible for Fella to live with both his families, going back and forth between Sophie's house and the Torreses' trailer—which suited Sammie and Sophie's boys just fine.

Sophie and Nate would watch Sancho too while Tanner and Lucie flew to Cancún for their honeymoon, the wedding gift from Vita and her new husband, Barry, who stood together watching the cake proceedings, laughing and applauding.

The photographer finished shooting the cake photos and Lucie and Tanner moved to the center of the room. Maria and others in the Bible study groups had donated a piñata for the children at the wedding reception.

With arms around each other's waists, Lucie and Tanner watched the merriment as the blindfolded children took turns, whacking at the bright yellow piñata shaped like a donkey.

Then Lucie let out a whoop as her mother let Miguel drag her to the center and insisted she take a turn with the bat. Blindfolded, Dorothy swung and swung again, each time missing the piñata. Miguel shouted directions, "Señora Dorothy, to the right! Now the left!"

Normally quiet Dorothy was laughing and jumping up and down.

Lucie shook with laughter. Where had her shy, unassuming mother, the perfect pastor's wife, vanished?

Tanner bent low and kissed Lucie.

As she moved her lips over her new husband's, she thought of the first day they'd met, and then she looked around the room with a smile. What wonders God had wrought!

* * * * *

Dear Reader,

Did you guess that I named my heroine for a fifties TV heroine? That's right, Lucie Hansen was inspired by Lucy Ricardo of *I Love Lucy*. Fortunately, my Lucie didn't get into as much "trouble" as her predecessor!

Opposites attract is an old axiom, but I think it remains true. I know my husband and I certainly prove it. He thinks in numbers and I in words! Our conversations are often filled with hilarious and sometimes maddening misunderstandings.

Tanner was a man committed to doing God's will, but he needed a petite live wire like Lucie to get him out of the church office and into the world. Lucie and Tanner were indeed a match made in heaven.

By the way, over the years, I've had many friends who were wives of pastors. God bless them. They don't get paid a salary, but devote their lives to their families and to their churches. Next Sunday, give your pastor's wife a hug!

I'd like to hear from you. Drop me a line or an e-mail.

Lyn Cote

Lyn Cote
P.O. Box 273
Hiawatha, IA 52233

www.booksbylyncote.com

Love Inspired

CROSSROADS

BY

IRENE HANNON

Being sent to the principal's office takes on a new meaning for single mom Tess Lockwood... especially when she sets eyes on rugged ex-cop-turned-educator Mitch Jackson. As they work together to keep Tess's teenage son from the wrong crowd, will they learn that God has brought them together to teach them the lesson of love?

Don't miss

CROSSROADS
On sale October 2003

Available at your favorite retail outlet.